Dirty Bertie

Bertie

SLIME and GRIME

DAVID ROBERTS WRITTEN BY **ALAN MACDONALD**

stripes

Collect all the
Dirty Bertie books!

Contents

STRIPES PUBLISHING LIMITED
An imprint of the Little Tiger Group
1 The Coda Studios, 189 Munster Road,
London SW6 6AW

A paperback original
First published in Great Britain in 2019

Characters created by David Roberts
Text copyright © Alan MacDonald
Fame! 2016 · Horror! 2014 · Aliens! 2015
Illustrations copyright © David Roberts
Fame! 2016 · Horror! 2014 · Aliens! 2015

ISBN: 978-1-78895-043-5

Printed and bound in the UK

10 9 8 7 6 5 4 3 2 1

Dirty Bertie

FAME!

For David ~ D R

For Cameron and Ben ~ A M

Contents

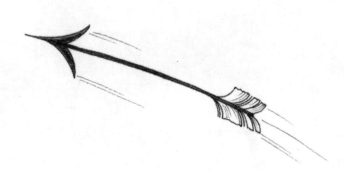

CHAPTER 1

Bertie plodded downstairs. He could hear his parents talking in the kitchen.

"That was Miss Lavish from the drama group on the phone," said Dad. "She says a company are looking for boys to come to an audition."

"For a play?" said Mum.

"No, it's something on TV," said Dad.

TV? Bertie skidded into the kitchen. He'd always wanted to be on TV and this could be his big chance!

"TV? Where? When?" he gabbled.

Dad groaned. He hadn't realized Bertie had been listening.

"This Saturday," he said. "But before you ask, I'm working so I can't take you."

"But it's *TV!*" said Bertie. "I'd be on TV!"

"I'm sure they'll get hundreds of boys applying," said Mum.

"Yes, but no one like ME!" argued Bertie.

"No, probably not," admitted Mum.

"Anyway, we don't know what it's for," said Dad. "It might just be a schools programme."

"Well I *go* to school, I'd be perfect!" said Bertie. "Pleeease!"

Dirty Bertie

"But who's going to take you?" asked Mum. "I can't. Suzy's got a dance class."

"I've *got* to go, I can't miss this!" wailed Bertie.

Mum had an idea. "What about Gran? I suppose she might take him?"

"She might," said Dad.

"YESSSSSS!" yelled Bertie, dancing round the room. "I'm going to be on TV!"

Dirty Bertie

Gran thought a TV audition sounded thrilling. She said she'd be delighted to take Bertie. So on Saturday morning they joined a long queue of boys and their parents at Central Studios. Mum was right – Bertie wasn't the only boy who wanted to be on TV. He scowled at his rivals, who were all dressed in their best clothes. Their faces were scrubbed clean and their hair shone like sunlight.

Dirty Bertie

Gran frowned at Bertie. "What's that on your face?" she said. "It looks like jam."

Bertie wriggled away as she tried to wipe it off with a tissue.

Gran sighed. Bertie looked as grubby and scruffy as ever.

"I wonder what sort of part it is," she said. "Maybe they'll want you to sing."

"Let's hope not," grunted Bertie. People usually covered their ears when he sang. But he did have acting experience. Last Christmas he'd played a dog in the musical *Oliver!* Everyone said it was a brilliant performance – apart from the bit when he'd brought down the scenery, but that could have happened to anyone.

CHAPTER 2

Two hours later, it was finally Bertie's turn to audition. They were shown into a room to meet Amy the director and her assistant, Paul.

"So, who have we got next?" asked Paul, checking his list. "Benny?"

"*Bertie*," said Bertie.

"What kind of TV show is it?" asked

Gran excitedly.

"It's an advert actually," explained Paul.

An *advert*! Bertie thought he'd be brilliant – he knew loads of adverts off by heart! And if it was an advert for sweets or chocolate he was willing to eat loads of them.

"I've done acting," he said. "I played a dog." He stuck out his tongue and panted, doing his best dog impression.

"Very good," said Amy. "But what we want is a boy who can be himself on camera."

"*I* can be myself," said Bertie. He was himself all the time – although usually it got him into trouble.

"Great," said Amy. She noticed Bertie's jam-stained face and wild hair. "Actually, you might suit the part," she said. "You're not like all the others we've seen today. You don't mind getting wet, I suppose?"

Bertie shook his head. It seemed like an odd question. Maybe it was raining in the advert. Or perhaps he'd be standing on a ship? If they needed a pirate captain, Bertie could do a brilliant accent.

"Just stand right here and read this line to the camera," said Paul.

Bertie took up his position and stared at the card Paul was holding.

"Mon-ster Bobbles for little mon-sters," he read.

"It's 'Monster Bubbles'," said Amy. "Try it again, with a bit more expression."

Bertie shut one eye. "AHARRRR! Monster Bubbles for little monsters!" he cried.

The director frowned. "What's with the funny voice?" she asked.

"I was being a pirate," Bertie told her. "I thought it'd make it more interesting."

"There aren't any pirates in this," said Amy. "Just stick to your normal voice."

"Be yourself," Gran reminded him.

Bertie thought being a pirate would be better, but he said the line again.

Amy nodded. "Thanks, that's great."

"Perfect," said Paul.

Bertie blinked. *Was that it?* Didn't they want to hear his other impressions? He could do teachers – Miss Boot on the warpath, for instance.

"Did I get the part?" he asked.

"We'll let you know," said Paul, showing them to the door. "Thanks for coming."

Outside, Bertie turned to Gran. "Well, that went pretty well I think," he said.

"Yes," agreed Gran. "If they want a one-eyed pirate with jam on his face, you're a certainty."

Dirty Bertie

The following week Bertie arrived home from school to find Gran in the kitchen clutching a letter addressed to him. He tore open the envelope and read the first few lines.

"I GOT IT!" he yelled. "WAHOOO! I got the part!"

Suzy gaped. Gran hugged him. Dad looked like he might faint.

"Seriously?" he said.

"See for yourself," said Bertie, handing over the letter. There it was in black and white. The TV company wanted Bertie at the studios next Saturday to film the advert.

"I told you!" grinned Bertie. He didn't see why his family looked so surprised. The TV people obviously knew talent when they saw it.

"What kind of advert is it?" asked Mum.

"I'm not exactly sure," said Gran.

"If they chose Bertie, it must be for air freshener," scoffed Suzy.

"Very funny," said Bertie. "Just because you're too ugly for TV!"

Gran tried to remember. "It was something about bubbles," she said. "Maybe it's a fizzy drink?"

Dirty Bertie

"Brilliant!" said Bertie. He loved fizzy
drinks and held the class record for the
longest burp. Anyway, who cared what
the advert was for! What mattered was
that he was going to appear on TV.
Wait till his friends heard about this –
they were going to be mad with envy!

"YOU? On *TV*?" said Darren, the next day.

"In your dreams," said Eugene.

"It's true," insisted Bertie. "I went to
this audition and they picked me for an
advert."

"Course they did," jeered Darren. "And they're paying you a million pounds."

"Maybe," said Bertie. "But it'll definitely be on TV."

His friends stared at him. "Seriously? A real advert – on *television*?" said Eugene.

"That's what I keep telling you!" said Bertie.

"Wow!" said Darren. "So what kind of advert?"

Bertie shrugged. "Dunno. It's probably some sort of fizzy drink," he said.

"Cool!" said Darren. "You'll be famous."

"I know!" said Bertie, grinning. "*World* famous!"

And this was just the beginning, he

Dirty Bertie

thought. When the advert went out,
everyone would want his autograph.
Miss Boot would have to call him "Sir".
Know-All Nick would bow when Bertie
walked into class. Being on TV was
going to be the best thing that had ever
happened to him!

CHAPTER 3

On Saturday morning Bertie and Gran
arrived at the TV studios. Bertie was so
excited he could hardly keep still. He
had been practising fizzy pop burps all
week.

A girl called Ellie met them and took
them along to a dressing room. Bertie
sat in a leather chair while she started

work on his make-up.

"I did tell him to wash his face this morning," sighed Gran.

"Don't worry," laughed Ellie. "The dirtier the better."

She was smearing Bertie's face with mud-coloured make-up. He looked like he'd just crawled out of a bog.

Gran looked puzzled. "Isn't he supposed to look smart?" she asked.

"Not for *this* advert." Ellie smiled. "He's meant to be as filthy as possible, otherwise he wouldn't need a bath."

Bertie sat up in his seat. Had he heard right? "A BATH?" he said.

"Yes, the advert's for bubble bath, didn't they tell you?" asked Ellie.

Bertie blinked. *Bubble bath?* Of course … that's what "Monster Bubbles" meant!

But wait a minute … surely they didn't expect him to…

"I'm not – you know – actually *in* the bath?" he gulped.

"Of course!" laughed Ellie. "But don't worry, there'll be plenty of bubbles to cover you."

Bertie turned pale. Why hadn't anyone warned him?

He couldn't appear on TV *in the bath*! He wouldn't be wearing socks or a vest … or anything!

Dirty Bertie

Finally it was time for Bertie's big scene. He waited nervously as the bath was prepared.

"I don't see why you're making such a big fuss," sighed Gran. "You have baths at home."

"Not often," said Bertie. "And not on TV!"

"But there'll be lots of bubbles," said Gran. "No one's going to see anything!"

"They'll see ME!" moaned Bertie. "You do it, if it's so easy!"

"I don't think anyone wants to see me in the bath!" giggled Gran.

Amy came over. "Ready, Bertie?" she asked.

Bertie swallowed. He hadn't minded

acting the first scene. All he'd had to do was walk in looking filthy from playing football – that came naturally. It was the bath scene he was dreading. Under his bathrobe he wore a tiny pair of pink pants. Ellie claimed no one would see them.

"Couldn't I keep the dressing gown on?" he begged.

"Not in the bath," said Amy. "What's up? Don't tell me you're embarrassed?"

"Course not." Bertie blushed. He looked at Gran for help, but she just shrugged her shoulders. It was too late to back out now.

"Come on," said Amy. "Just get in the bath and say the line. It's simple!"

Easy for you to say, thought Bertie. *You're not wearing pink pants.*

Dirty Bertie

"Right, stand by everyone!" called Amy.

The filming started. Bertie's TV mum ran the taps, making clouds of bubbles.

"And action, Bertie!" said Amy.

Bertie dropped the bathrobe. Taking a run, he dived into the bath head first…

Water flew everywhere, soaking Amy and all the camera crew.

SPLOOSH!

Dirty Bertie

"Monster-bubblesh for li'l monsters!" burbled Bertie, from beneath a mountain of suds.

Amy wiped her eye. "Right," she said. "Let's try that again shall we, Bertie? And this time can we actually see your face?"

CHAPTER 4

Weeks passed. Bertie hoped that his starring TV role had been forgotten. Perhaps the advert wasn't going to be shown after all? When his friends asked questions, he mumbled excuses and changed the subject. But one Friday it arrived – a letter from the TV company. Bertie opened it and groaned.

"What is it?" asked Mum.

"Er … nothing," said Bertie.

"It can't be nothing, let me see," said Mum. She read through the letter.

"But that's fantastic, Bertie!" she said. "Your advert's going out on Friday."

Bertie nodded glumly.

"Well, aren't you pleased?" asked Mum. "You're going to be on TV!"

"Mmm," said Bertie. "I'm just not feeling too well."

He still hadn't told anyone the terrible truth about the advert. His family had no idea and nor did anyone at school. Only Gran knew – and he'd made her promise to keep it a secret.

"Well, I can't wait to see it," said Mum.

"Nor me," said Suzy. "My smelly little brother on TV! We should invite Gran round to watch."

"Yes, and the Nicelys too," said Mum. "I'm sure Angela would love to see it."

"No, not Angela!" groaned Bertie. If she heard about it, the news would be all round school. He didn't want *anyone* to see the advert.

The following evening Bertie's lounge was crowded with people. Despite his protests, Mum had invited Gran, Darren, Eugene and the Nicelys from next door. They were all eager to see Bertie's big moment on TV.

Bertie felt sick. Just as he'd feared,

Angela had blabbed about it to
everyone. Even Miss Boot was going to
watch. He stared at the TV. Perhaps
they'd got the date wrong? Or maybe
a sudden power cut would save him.
Actually, that wasn't a bad idea…

"Isn't it exciting!" said Mum.

"Who'd have thought it? Bertie on
TV," said Dad.

"Aren't *you* excited, Bertie?" cooed
Angela, moving closer to him.

"Not really," said Bertie, sneaking out a
hand for the remote.

ZAP! The TV went blank.

"What's happened?" gasped Gran.

"Oh no, a power cut," sighed Bertie.

"It's not a power cut, you're sitting
on the remote, you idiot," said Darren.
"Give it here."

Dirty Bertie

"Get off!" cried Bertie. A brief tug-of-war broke out, ending with Mum grabbing the remote and turning the TV back on.

The adverts were just starting. Bertie could only watch through his fingers. "Please, please, don't let them show it," he prayed.

"This is it!" cried Gran.

Bertie peeped out. There he was on the screen, covered in mud and holding a football.

"So *that's* why they chose you!" said Mum.

The scene changed to the bathroom.

Dirty Bertie

Taps were running as Bertie's TV mum poured in bubble bath.

Here it comes, thought Bertie.

ARGH! There he was, wearing nothing but bubbles! The camera zoomed in... "Monster Bubbles for little monsters!"

Darren fell about laughing. "Ha ha ha! You didn't say you were in the bath!"

"Hee hee! Bertie's in the nuddy!" sang Eugene.

"Shut up! I was wearing pants!" moaned Bertie, turning pink.

"Well, I think you did very well, Bertie," said Gran.

Angela nodded. "I thought you were fantastic!"

"Yes, and at least you got a bath," laughed Dad.

Bertie zapped off the TV.

"Okay, you've all seen it," he groaned. "Now can we just forget about it?"

Suzy grinned. "I wouldn't count on it," she said. "Adverts are on every day – they could be showing it for months yet!"

MONTHS? Bertie looked horrified. This was terrible! He was never going on TV again – not even if they begged him!

FISHY!

CHAPTER 1

It was Saturday suppertime. Bertie was meant to be laying the table with Suzy. Dad came in carrying a large box.

"I thought I might go fishing tomorrow," he said.

Bertie looked up hopefully. "Fishing? Can I come?" he asked.

"YOU? You don't like fishing," said Dad.

Dirty Bertie

"I've never been," replied Bertie.

"Probably because your dad's never offered to take you," said Mum, folding her arms.

Dad raised his eyes to the ceiling. Taking Bertie anywhere was risky, but fishing was asking for trouble. He'd probably get covered in mud and fall in the river. Whatever happened, one thing was certain – if Bertie came along there wouldn't be a moment's peace.

Dirty Bertie

"You'd probably find it boring," said Dad. "Most of the time it's just sitting around."

"But don't you catch fish?" asked Bertie.

"Sometimes – if you're lucky," admitted Dad.

"I'd be good at fishing," said Bertie. "Remember when we got that goldfish?"

Suzy rolled her eyes. "That was at the funfair," she said.

All the same, Bertie was keen to go fishing. It sounded dead easy – you just dangled a hook in the water and pulled out a fish. Anyone could do it! Besides, anything that involved worms and maggots was his idea of heaven!

"Fishing's not that simple," argued Dad. "You have to learn how to cast a line."

"Surely you can teach him that?" said Mum. "I'd have thought you'd *want* to take your son fishing."

"I bet *other* dads take their sons," grumbled Bertie. "I bet they're *glad* to take them."

"Anyway, it would be nice for the two of you to do something together," said Mum.

Dad knew when he was beaten. "All right, all right, I'll take him," he groaned.

"YESSSSS!" cheered Bertie. "Can I borrow your fishing rod?"

"Certainly not, you'll break it," snapped Dad. "You can borrow my old fishing net."

Bertie supposed a net was better than nothing. He opened Dad's fishing box and examined the tins and boxes. He picked one up and took off the lid.

Dirty Bertie

"Woah! MAGGOTS!" he gasped. "Look, there's millions of them!"

"EWWW!" shrieked Suzy.

"ARGH! TAKE THEM AWAY!" screamed Mum with a shudder.

Dad grabbed the tin and closed the lid. "For goodness' sake, leave things alone, Bertie!" he cried.

Bertie shrugged. He didn't see why everyone was so touchy. It was only a few measly maggots after all. He wasn't planning on racing them on the kitchen table.

Dirty Bertie

He wiped his nose on his sleeve.
Tomorrow would be his first ever
fishing trip and he couldn't wait. Maybe
he would catch a real whopper – an
octopus or a great white shark. Imagine
the look on his friends' faces if he
brought one of *those* into school!

CHAPTER 2

The next morning, Bertie found Dad in the kitchen making sandwiches.

"You're not even dressed!" Dad moaned, glancing at the clock. "We need to get going!"

"I haven't had breakfast yet," grumbled Bertie.

"Well hurry up," said Dad, handing

him a plate. "If we don't get there early, we won't get a good spot."

Bertie couldn't see why they were in such a hurry. It was only half past eight! In any case, the fish weren't going anywhere – they were probably still in bed.

Dad dropped a couple of slices of bread into the toaster.

"Can't I have cereal?" asked Bertie.

"NO!" said Dad. "Just hurry up!"

Later that morning they arrived at the riverbank. Dad was anxious to claim his favourite fishing spot before anyone else got there. Bertie helped him carry their bags and boxes down to the river. There were quite a few fishermen out already.

Dad halted. "I knew it!" he groaned. "Someone's pinched our spot!"

"Where?" asked Bertie.

"There, under the trees," said Dad, pointing. "I always go there."

Bertie could see a man and a boy, sitting with their rods. They were both wearing floppy green hats — even so, the boy looked oddly familiar.

"Can't we tell them to move?" asked
Bertie.

"Don't be daft!" said Dad. "We'll just
have to find somewhere else."

They chose a spot a little way along
the river. Bertie grabbed his fishing net
and scrambled down the bank.

"Where are you going?" asked Dad.

"To catch a fish!" replied Bertie.

"We haven't set up yet!" said Dad.
"Help me unpack."

48

Dirty Bertie

Bertie sighed and clambered back up. He couldn't see why fishing needed so much stuff! There were hooks, reels and lines, not to mention tins of flies, worms and maggots.

He unfolded a chair. "*Now* can I go?" he begged.

"Fishing isn't something you can hurry," explained Dad. "It's all in the preparation. You can't just dive in and expect to catch a fish!"

Bertie didn't see why not.

He waded in with his net, until the water sloshed over the top of his wellies.

Dirty Bertie

"Oh no, not *you!*" said a reedy voice behind him.

Bertie swung round. Standing on the bank was Know-All Nick in a baggy coat and floppy green hat. Bertie stared open-mouthed. It was bad enough seeing Nick at school every day, without him turning up here.

"You've pinched our spot," complained Bertie.

"Tough luck! We were here first!" simpered Nick. "My dad *always* takes me fishing on Sundays."

"He must be bonkers," said Bertie. He was surprised that Nick wanted to go fishing, what with all the maggots and worms. At school Nick screamed if a fly came near him.

"My dad knows *everything* about fishing," bragged Nick. "We're going to catch a whopper!"

"Huh!" scoffed Bertie. "Fat chance!"

"That's what you think," said Nick. "*I've* got my own fishing rod!"

"Big deal," said Bertie. "I've got a net and that's better."

"I don't *think* so," sneered Nick. "You won't catch a flea with your smelly old net!"

"Want to bet?" said Bertie.

They were interrupted by their dads arriving. Nick's dad looked as pale and weedy as his son.

"I hope you two boys are getting on," he said.

"Of course," lied Nick. "Bertie was just

telling me that his net's better than my fishing rod."

"I don't know about that," laughed Nick's dad. "Have you done much fishing?"

"It's my first time," answered Bertie.

"Oh dear! Nicholas got his first fishing rod when he was five!" boasted Nick's dad.

Dirty Bertie

"Bertie's never been interested in fishing," said Dad.

"Yes, I have!" argued Bertie. "You never take me!"

Dad looked at the ground.

"Anyway, we'll leave you to it," chuckled Nick's dad. "Best of luck."

"Yes, let me know if you catch any tiddlers, Bertie. TEE HEE!" sniggered Nick.

Bertie watched them go. He would show that big know-all. He was going to catch the biggest fish in the river, then they'd see who was laughing.

CHAPTER 3

The river drifted slowly by. Bertie shivered in the wind. They'd been sitting for hours without any sign of a fish.

"Can't I go paddling?" he pleaded.

"No, I've told you," said Dad. "You'll frighten the fish away."

"What fish? There aren't any!" moaned Bertie.

Dirty Bertie

"Of course there are. Have a little patience," said Dad.

Bertie slumped back in his chair. He'd expected fishing to be a lot more exciting. He wasn't allowed to do anything! He couldn't throw stones, climb a tree or even swish his net in the river in case it frightened the fish.

"Isn't it lunchtime?" he nagged.

"Stop asking! It's only twelve o'clock!" sighed Dad.

"That *is* lunchtime," said Bertie. "I only had three slices of toast for breakfast."

"Okay, one sandwich," sighed Dad. "But don't wolf down the whole lot."

Bertie found the lunch box and took a sandwich. He glanced back at Nick and his dad – they looked like two garden gnomes clutching their fishing rods.

Dirty Bertie

Obviously Nick hadn't caught anything yet or he would have come over to gloat. *I wonder what he's got for lunch?* thought Bertie, as Dad catapulted a shower of maggots into the river. Suddenly a brilliant idea popped into Bertie's head. Maybe Nick would like a sandwich — a special *surprise sandwich*?

Bertie bent over the fishing box.

"What are you after?" asked Dad.

"Nothing! Just looking," said Bertie. He waited until Dad turned back to the river, then quickly grabbed a tin from the box. Inside was a sea of wriggling maggots.

Bertie took another
sandwich and scooped
in some juicy maggots,
hiding them under a slice
of cheese. It still looked like any ordinary
sandwich. He popped it back in the
box. Know-All Nick was in for a squirmy
surprise.

Bertie took the lunch box over to Nick at
the river's edge.

"Yum, yum!" he said, munching loudly.

Know-All Nick glared. "Do you have to
do that?" he grumbled.

"Fishing makes you hungry," said Bertie.
"Cheese and pickle's my favourite!"

Nick sniffed. "We've brought our own
sandwiches – carrot salad," he said.

57

Dirty Bertie

"YUCK! Not as nice as this," said Bertie. "Go on, try one."

He offered the lunch box. Nick frowned. It wasn't like Bertie to share his food. What was he up to?

"Have one!" urged Bertie.

Nick considered. Two could play at this game. "Okay, thanks," he said, taking the top sandwich.

Here goes, thought Bertie. *Wait till you taste my special surprise ingredient. Squirmy wormy maggots! Yum!*

Nick opened his mouth.

"Wait, I can't eat all this," he said, holding out the sandwich to Bertie. "Why don't we share it?"

Bertie's face fell. "WHAT?"

"Half each," said Nick. "It's only fair." He tore the sandwich in two and handed half to Bertie. "Eat up!" he said.

Bertie gulped, caught in his own trap.

"What's the matter? I thought cheese and pickle was your favourite?" jeered Nick.

"Um, yes," said Bertie. "But you go first."

"Oh no, after *you*," Nick insisted.

Bertie turned white. There was nothing for it. His stomach heaved. He slowly raised the squirmy sandwich to his lips and opened his mouth…

"Go on," crowed Nick.

"NICHOLAS! Lunchtime!" called Nick's dad.

Bertie breathed a sigh of relief.

Saved!

"Got to go," said Nick, handing back his half of the sandwich. "Here, you keep it."

Bertie stomped back to his dad. Rats! What a waste of a good sandwich! He put both halves back into the box and closed the lid. Maybe he'd get a chance to slip it into Nick's bag later…

CHAPTER 4

Dad was sipping a cup of coffee from his flask.

"How's your friend? Has he caught anything?" he asked.

"Know-All Nick? No chance!" snorted Bertie. He checked his own net, which he'd left lying in the shallows hoping a fish might jump into it. Empty. Bertie sighed.

Dirty Bertie

He had to catch something before Smugface beat him to it.

"Right, let's have something to eat," said Dad. "Where's the lunch box?"

Bertie handed it over and got out some crisps. Dad took the top sandwich. "That's funny," he frowned. "Did you cut these in half?"

"No," said Bertie. He looked up. Wait! The maggot sandwich… Hadn't he put it back in the box?

"STOP!" yelled Bertie.

Too late. Dad took a bite. "What's the matter?" he asked.

Bertie shook his head. Dad chewed for a moment, then pulled a face.

"This tastes funny, sort of salty," he said. "I'm sure they were all cheese and pickle."

Dirty Bertie

"They were… I mean, they are," stammered Bertie.

But Dad had opened the sandwich to check inside. His eyes bulged. His tongue came out.

"MAGGOTS!" he croaked, clutching his throat. "It's got maggots in it!"

Dirty Bertie

"Yikes!" said Bertie. "How did they get in there?"

Dad spat out the sandwich on the grass.

"PLUGH! UGH! BLECH!"

Honestly, thought Bertie, *it's only a few maggots.* Dad sounded as if he was dying.

"DID YOU DO THIS?" cried Dad, waving the half-eaten sandwich.

"M-ME?" said Bertie.

"Who else?" snapped Dad. "You put maggots in here, didn't you?"

Bertie looked guilty. "Not on purpose! It was meant for Nick!" he wailed. "How was I to know YOU were going to eat it?"

Dad hurled the maggot sandwich into the river with a howl of rage.

Dirty Bertie

"That's it," he fumed. "I feel sick! We're going home."

"But Dad…" said Bertie.

"No buts, I knew this was a bad idea," said Dad.

"But Dad!" cried Bertie, pointing to the river. "LOOK!"

The maggot sandwich was bobbing around like a cork on the water. Dad jumped to his feet. It could only mean one thing…

"A FISH!" he yelled. "Quick! Where's my rod?"

But Bertie didn't wait. He sploshed into the river and plunged in his net. When he scooped it out, there was something flapping in the bottom – a big silver fish.

"WOW! A WHOPPER!" gasped Bertie.

Dad helped him haul the fish into the shallows, where they emptied it into a larger net.

"That's a carp!" said Dad. "A monster too!"

"I told you!" grinned Bertie. "I told you I'd catch one!"

The noise brought Nick and his dad running over. When Nick saw Bertie's prize catch, he could hardly believe it.

"You caught that?" he said. "But … but how?"

"With my smelly old net, how do you think?" said Bertie.

"Good heavens!" said Nick's dad, impressed.

"Beginner's luck," sneered Nick.

Dad shook his head. "Oh, I don't think luck had anything to do with it," he said.

Dirty Bertie

"No," grinned Bertie. "The secret of fishing is you just need the right sandwiches!"

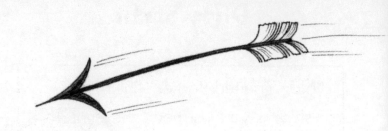

OUTLAW!

CHAPTER 1

TWANG!

Bertie's imaginary bow sent an arrow winging into the sky. He was Robin Hood, the fearless outlaw, wanted dead or alive. This morning Miss Boot had read to her class from *The Tales of Robin Hood,* and for once Bertie had stopped yawning and listened. Robin Hood lived

Dirty Bertie

in the forest with his merry men and spent his time robbing the rich to give to the poor. This was the life, thought Bertie – he was *born* to lead a gang of outlaws.

"Follow me, men!" he cried. "Let's find someone rich who wants robbing!"

"Okay, Robin!" said Darren-the-Dale.

"Who shall we ambush?" asked Eugene Scarlet.

Bertie looked around the playground for a likely victim. Over on a bench sat a pale-faced boy munching an apple. Aha! The evil Sheriff of *Nick*ingham – Know-All Nick! The outlaws crept closer, silent as mice. On Bertie's signal, they leaped out, taking aim with their imaginary bows and arrows.

"SURRENDER!" yelled Bertie.

Know-All Nick almost choked on his apple. "URGH! Heeelp!" he squawked.

"I am Robin Hood," cried Bertie. "And these are my brave outlaws. Turn out your pockets!"

Dirty Bertie

"Push off!" said Know-All Nick.

"Right, don't say we didn't warn you," said Bertie. "Take him prisoner, men."

Nick leaped to his feet. "You touch me and I'll scream," he warned. "Miss Boot doesn't like fighting in the playground."

Bertie frowned. He knew Miss Boot was on playground patrol today and Nick's screams would bring her running. Rats! Maybe they'd have to rob the cowardly sheriff another day...

Dirty Bertie

Over by the fence, Angela Nicely was skipping with her friends. The outlaws sneaked up behind them.

"YAHAAAAA! SURRENDER!" yelled Bertie.

Angela stopped skipping. "Hello, Bertie. Are you playing pirates?"

"Course not. I'm Robin Hood and we are the outlaws of Sherbet Forest," said Bertie.

Angela clapped her hands. "Goodie! Can *I* be Robin Hood?" she begged.

"No chance," said Bertie. "There's only one Robin Hood and that's me. We arm-wrestled for it and I won."

"Okay then, I'll be an outlaw," offered Angela.

"You can't," said Bertie. "We don't have girls in our gang."

Dirty Bertie

Angela stepped a little closer, fluttering her eyelashes.

"Pleeease, Bertie!" she cooed.

Bertie gulped. He hadn't forgotten the time Angela had chased him round the playground trying to kiss him. What if she did it again in front of his friends? There was only one thing to do…

"RUN!" cried Bertie.

Dirty Bertie

The brave outlaws fled round the corner.

"This is hopeless," panted Bertie. "I bet Robin Hood never had this trouble."

"Maybe we should take it in turns robbing each other?" suggested Eugene.

"That's no good, we've got to rob the rich – that's what they did in the story," argued Darren.

"Exactly," agreed Bertie. "There's got to be *someone* worth robbing."

He looked around, trying to think. "I know – Royston Rich!" he cried. Royston was the biggest show off in the class. He came to school every day in his dad's sports car and he was always bragging about the swimming pool in his garden. If anyone deserved to be set on by outlaws it was Royston!

CHAPTER 2

Bertie and his gang sneaked across the playground. They found Royston behind the boys' toilets, cramming a chocolate bar into his mouth. On Bertie's signal, the outlaws jumped out.

"HANDS UP! SURRENDER!" yelled Bertie, waving a stick he'd picked up.

Royston wiped his mouth. "What do

you want?" he groaned.

"We're outlaws," Darren told him.

"You fooled me," jeered Royston.

"Well, I'm Robin Hood and this is a robbery," said Bertie. "Hand over your gold."

"I don't have any gold, stupid," replied Royston.

"Then hand over your chocolate," said Darren.

"Please," added Eugene.

"Or else," said Bertie.

Royston folded his arms. "Or else what?" he said. "You're all going to wet your pants?"

Bertie poked his stick into Royston's chest. But Royston grabbed it and snapped the stick in half, throwing it on the ground.

"Huh! Some outlaws you are," he sneered. "You couldn't rob my little sister!" He walked off, treading on Bertie's foot as he passed.

"That went well," said Eugene.

"Why didn't you stop him?" grumbled Bertie.

"You're Robin Hood, *you* stop him," said Darren.

Bertie rolled his eyes. This was getting them nowhere – Know-All Nick had got away, Angela had tried to join them and now Royston Rich had made them look stupid! How could they be outlaws if they couldn't manage a simple robbery?

"We'll get him later," said Bertie. "He always goes to the sweet shop after school. We'll wait outside and nab his sweets."

Eugene frowned. "Can't we be good outlaws?" he asked. "My mum says it's wrong to steal."

"It's not stealing, it's robbing the rich," said Bertie.

"Same thing," said Eugene.

"No, it's not," argued Bertie. "Robin

Hood robbed the rich and Miss Boot said he's a legend."

"Yes," said Eugene, "but he gave to the poor."

"That's what we're doing too," said Bertie. "Royston's loaded and he always has tons of sweets. We're just helping him to share them out."

"Exactly," said Darren. "That way it's fairer for everyone."

Eugene shrugged. When you put it like that, it was hard to argue. "But what if we get caught?" he worried.

"We won't," said Bertie. "We'll disguise ourselves as outlaws so he won't know who we are."

CHAPTER 3

After school the outlaws hurried to the sweet shop. They hid behind a wall and waited for Royston Rich to appear. All three had hankies tied over their faces, which Bertie claimed was an old outlaw trick.

"Here he comes," whispered Darren. "Keep down."

Dirty Bertie

Royston pushed open the door
and went into the sweet shop. A few
minutes later, he came out clasping a
bag and cramming sweets into his mouth
three at a time.

"Now!" whispered Bertie.

"YAHAAAAA!" The masked outlaws
swarmed forward, surrounding Royston.

"Surrender or die!" yelled Bertie.

Dirty Bertie

Royston clutched the bag to his chest. The leader of the outlaws had a dirty face half hidden by a grubby hanky. It could only be one person.

"Bertie!" cried Royston.

"No, it's not," lied Bertie. "Hand over the sweets."

"No way," said Royston. "I'm not scared of you lot."

"Okay, you asked for it," said Bertie. "Tickle him!"

The outlaws advanced, fingers at the ready.

"No, please! I'm not ticklish!" squawked Royston, backing away. "Ha ha! Hee hee!"

He squirmed and wriggled, dropping the bag of sweets on the ground.

Dirty Bertie

Bertie scooped it up, waving the bag in the air.

"Got it!" he cried. "Come on, men, back to Sherbet Forest!"

The outlaws ran off down the road, whooping in triumph.

"I'll get you for this, Bertie!" howled Royston. "I'm telling on you!"

Dirty Bertie

Back at the park, the outlaws hid in their secret forest camp near the playground.

Eugene looked around anxiously. "Now we're for it," he said. "Royston knows who we are."

"Stop worrying," said Bertie. "Have a liquorice torpedo."

They all helped themselves from Royston's bag.

"So anyway, who shall we share them with?" asked Eugene.

"*Share* them?" said Darren.

"Yes, you know, robbing the rich to give to the poor," Eugene reminded them. "Like Robin Hood."

"That's right," said Bertie, sucking a lemon sherbet. "If we're going to be outlaws we've got to do it properly. The question is, who deserves a share of the sweets?"

"What about Donna?" suggested Darren.

"She's not poor!" scoffed Bertie.

"Trevor then."

"He's a vegetarian, they don't eat sweets," said Darren.

"Well, who then?" asked Eugene.

Bertie frowned. It was complicated. If they shared the sweets with one of their friends, then it wasn't fair on all the others. They could always divide them equally – but then there wouldn't be enough to go round.

"Let's go back to my house," suggested Bertie. "We can decide later."

The outlaws agreed that this was a

good plan and set off, passing round
the sweets as they went.

Ten minutes later they reached Bertie's
house and paused at the gate.

"Better hide the bag," warned Darren.
"Your mum will ask where we got all
these sweets."

"Good thinking," said Bertie,
but looking in the bag,
his face fell. "There's not
that many left," he said.

"WHAT? How many?"
asked Eugene.

Bertie counted. "Four."

"FOUR!" cried Darren.
"That can't be right – who's
scoffed them all?"

"I guess we did," admitted Bertie.

They had certainly helped themselves to one or two sweets at the park ... then one or two more on the way home. Possibly it might have been six or seven.

Eugene rolled his eyes. "But what about sharing them with the poor?" he moaned.

"Four sweets aren't going to go far," said Bertie.

"No," agreed Darren. "Four's hardly worth keeping."

Bertie emptied them out into his hand.

"Might as well eat them," he said. "One each and I'll save one for Whiffer."

They finished off the last of the sweets. On the whole Bertie thought they'd acted pretty fairly. He was almost certain Robin Hood would have done the same thing.

CHAPTER 4

Next morning, the three outlaws trooped into school. Royston Rich was waiting for them in the playground.

"Right, fat face, where's my sweets?" he demanded.

Bertie frowned. "What sweets?" he asked.

"You know what sweets – the ones

you stole from me yesterday," said Royston. "If I don't get them back, I'm telling Miss Boot."

"You wouldn't!" said Eugene.

"Just watch me," said Royston.

They filed into class. A minute later Miss Boot swept into the room, scattering the class to their desks.

"Sit down and no talking," she barked.

Royston gave Bertie a goofy smile. He stood up and raised his hand.

Uh oh, now we're for it, thought Bertie.

"Miss Boot," whined Royston. "Bertie and his friends took my sweets!"

"I said, 'NO talking'!" snapped Miss Boot.

Dirty Bertie

"But Miss—" began Royston.

"QUIET!" boomed Miss Boot. "I am not interested in silly tales about sweets. I've told you before you're NOT to bring them to school. Anyone caught eating sweets will have me to deal with. DO I MAKE MYSELF CLEAR?"

Royston nodded and sat down sulkily. He scowled at Bertie. This wasn't over yet – not by a long way.

At break time Bertie and his friends charged out into the playground. Royston marched up to them.

"Fat lot of good that did," crowed Bertie. "Serves you right for telling tales."

"Never mind that," said Royston. "You've got to help me."

Dirty Bertie

Checking that no one was looking, he brought out a paper bag. Inside were three pale blue gobstoppers, as big as golf balls.

"Where did you get those?" gasped Darren.

"From the sweet shop this morning," said Royston. "But what am I going to do? You heard what Miss Boot said – no sweets in school."

"I'd hate to be in your shoes if she catches you," said Eugene. "Better hide them quickly."

"Yes, but *where*?" moaned Royston.

Bertie eyed the gobstoppers and licked his lips. This was too good to be true.

"We could hide them for you if you like," he offered.

"*Really?* Would you?" said Royston gratefully.

Bertie shrugged. "No problem," he said. "I'm sure we'll think of something."

"Anything!" said Royston. "Just don't let Miss Boot see them or I'm dead!"

He handed over the bag and hurried off, looking pleased with himself.

"Are you mad?" Darren asked Bertie. "Where are we going to hide three huge gobstoppers?"

Bertie raised his eyebrows. "Where do you think?" he said, reaching into the bag.

When the bell went they all trooped back into class. Royston Rich turned round and gave Bertie a goofy grin. Bertie frowned. He didn't see what Royston was so pleased about. He wouldn't be seeing those giant gobstoppers again.

But as the lesson started, Bertie noticed that the three of them were attracting some funny looks. *What was going on?*

He nudged Darren. "Have I got something on my face?" he whispered.

Darren looked at him. "YIKES! Your lips – they're bright blue!" he hissed.

Dirty Bertie

Bertie stared. "So are yours!" he gasped. "And Eugene's too!"

All three of them had bright blue lips with blue tongues to match. They looked like weird aliens! But how had it happened? Bertie groaned. The gobstoppers! That sneaky rat Royston had tricked them into eating joke sweets. If Miss Boot ever found out, they were in BIG trouble. Bertie slid down in his seat.

"BERTIE!" barked Miss Boot. "SIT UP STRAIGHT! What are you doing?"

"Nuffink!" mumbled Bertie.

"Speak up!" snapped Miss Boot. "And take your hand away from your mouth when you're talking."

Slowly Bertie removed his hand. Miss Boot stared at his bright blue lips. Then she noticed Darren and Eugene.

Dirty Bertie

There could only be one explanation…

"SWEETS!" thundered Miss Boot. "You've been eating sweets! Come out to the front, all of you!"

Bertie groaned. They'd probably be picking up litter in the playground for the rest of their lives. That did it, he thought. No more Robin Hood or robbing the rich. Starting tomorrow he was going back to the quiet life of a pirate.

Dirty Bertie
HORROR!

For Emma, who has been a star editor

~ D R and A M

Contents

CHAPTER 1

Gran was round at Bertie's house.
She seemed pleased with herself for
some reason.

"Notice anything different?" she said.

"New dress?" asked Dad.

"New shoes?" asked Mum.

"You've got fatter," said Bertie.

"I have not!" snapped Gran. "If you

103

must know, I've had my hair done."

Bertie stared. It was true. Gran's hair was normally white and frizzy, but today it was blonde and frizzy.

"I wanted to look smart for the cinema," she said.

"The cinema?" cried Bertie. "Can I come?"

"You?" said Gran.

"Yes, they're showing *Return of the Blob Thing*," said Bertie. "Darren says it's meant to be well scary."

"It doesn't sound suitable," said Mum. "Anyway, I'm sure Gran doesn't want to see a scary film."

Gran smiled. "Well, I'd have to ask Reg," she said, blushing a little.

"Reg? Who's Reg?" asked Dad.

"My new boyfriend," giggled Gran.

Dirty Bertie

"Tomorrow's our first date."

Boyfriend? Bertie almost choked on his biscuit. Should Gran be getting a boyfriend at her age? Next she'd be wearing jeans and getting her nose pierced!

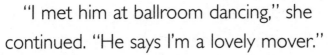

"I met him at ballroom dancing," she continued. "He says I'm a lovely mover."

"Does he now?" said Dad. "And he's taking you on a date?"

"That's right," said Gran. "He's quite the charmer. I think he fancies me, Bertie." She burst into a fit of giggles.

Bertie didn't know where to look. What had got into her? Gran wasn't normally like this – she sounded like a fourteen-year-old!

"What were you saying about a film, Bertie?" said Gran.

"Oh no, that's okay," said Bertie quickly. "You go with whatshisname."

The last thing he wanted was a cinema trip with Gran and her boyfriend. How embarrassing! What if they held hands during the film? What if they put their arms round each other and… No, he didn't even want to think about it.

While Gran was upstairs in the loo, Dad turned to Bertie. "Maybe you *should* go to the cinema tomorrow," he said.

"Me? No way!" said Bertie.

"But I thought you wanted to go?"

"Not with Gran and her boyfriend!"

Dad sighed. "The problem is, we don't know anything about this Reg," he said. "He could be after her money."

"Really?" said Bertie. He didn't know Gran had any money!

"What I mean is, he could be anybody," said Dad. "He might be a crook … or a kidnapper!"

"Don't be silly," scoffed Mum. "She met him at ballroom dancing."

"Oh well, that's all right, then!" said Dad, rolling his eyes. "All I'm saying is, Bertie could keep an eye on her."

Dirty Bertie

"Why me? If you're so worried, YOU go!" said Bertie.

"I can't go, she's my mother!" said Dad. He brought out his wallet. "Look, how much is the cinema?" he asked. "Here's five pounds."

Bertie hesitated. He would much rather see the film with his friends. But this might be his only chance.

"Can I see *Return of the Blob Thing*?" he asked.

"I don't see why not," said Dad.

"Only if Gran thinks it's suitable," said Mum.

Gran was coming back. "Don't tell her I put you up to this," whispered Dad.

Bertie stuffed the money into his pocket. Result!

CHAPTER 2

"You jammy dodger!" said Darren on the way to school the next day. "How did you fix that?"

Bertie shrugged. "It was easy. Dad's actually paying me to go."

"I wish my mum would let me go," said Eugene. "She says I'm not old enough for scary films."

"My dad says the cinema costs too much," sighed Darren. "Who's taking you, anyway?"

Bertie looked uncomfortable. "Actually it's my gran – and her boyfriend," he admitted.

"HER BOYFRIEND!" Darren burst out laughing. "Ha ha! Seriously?"

"You *are* joking?" said Eugene.

"It'll be fine," said Bertie.

"I wouldn't bet on it," said Darren. "Are they in love?"

"NO!" cried Bertie. "It's the first time they've gone out."

"That's even worse," said Darren. "My mum made my sister and her boyfriend take me to the cinema once. As soon as the lights went down they started, you know ... kissing."

Dirty Bertie

"EWW!" cried Eugene.

"This is my gran!" said Bertie. "She's about ninety!"

"Exactly," said Darren. "Imagine seeing your gran kissing in the cinema. Gross!"

Bertie didn't want to imagine it. There was no way he wanted to be there if Gran and her boyfriend were getting all smoochy. He'd be having nightmares about it for months!

Dirty Bertie

If Bertie had his way, old people wouldn't be allowed to go on dates, they'd stick to knitting and bingo. But he'd promised to go now. He'd just have to make sure that Gran and Reg didn't get any ideas.

The next evening, Bertie arrived at Gran's house. As usual Gran hadn't finished getting ready. She was still in her petticoat and fluffy slippers.

She held two dresses against her in turn for him to inspect. "What do you think, Bertie?" she asked. "The green one … or the red? Which goes better with my hair?"

"I don't care!" groaned Bertie, covering his eyes. "Just put something on!"

Gran went off to get changed and put on her make-up. Bertie thought she was going to a lot of trouble for a trip to the cinema.

DING-DONG!

"That'll be Reg," said Gran, hurrying out. "How do I look?"

"At least you're dressed," said Bertie.

Gran opened the front door. Reg was wearing a checked jacket and a yellow scarf knotted round his neck. He'd

Dirty Bertie

tried to hide his bald patch by combing
over what was left of his hair. If Gran
reckoned he was good looking, she
needed her eyes tested, thought Bertie.

"Dotty! Don't you look a picture!"
cried Reg, coming in.

Bertie stood there scowling, his arms
folded.

"And who's this young man?" asked
Reg.

"This is Bertie, my grandson," said
Gran. "I told you he might be coming."

"Oh. I thought you were joking," said
Reg. He bent down to Bertie's level.
"Wouldn't you rather be with your little
friends?" he asked.

"None of them are allowed to come,"
said Bertie.

"Well, I hope you're going to behave,"
said Reg. "Mind you, I can't promise the
same for me and Dotty."

"Oh stop it, Reg!" hooted Gran.

Bertie rolled his eyes. If they were
going to carry on like this all night, he
might have to wear a bag over his head.

They squeezed into Reg's tiny car
and drove to the cinema. Bertie had

to squash in the back. Reg's aftershave stunk the car out, and he kept looking in the driver's mirror to check his hair. Gran did her best to laugh at his terrible jokes.

At least when the film started Reg would have to shut up, thought Bertie.

CHAPTER 3

There was a long queue at the box office when they arrived. The multiplex was showing eight films on different screens.

"Can I get some popcorn?" asked Bertie. "And a slushy?"

"Go on then," said Gran.

"My treat," said Reg. "Take your time, we'll be in the queue."

Dirty Bertie

Bertie hurried off. He chose the Giant Whopper popcorn that came in a huge bucket, and a bright red strawberry slushy. He carried them across the foyer, spilling popcorn as he went. On the way he spotted a poster.

Bertie couldn't wait. He hurried back to join Gran and Reg.

"It's showing on Screen 4," he told them, excitedly.

"What is?" asked Gran.

"The film, of course... *Return of the Blob Thing*," said Bertie.

"You're too late," said Reg. "We've just bought tickets for this one."

He pointed at a poster above them. The film was called *Me, You and Bonzo Too*. The poster showed a smiling couple cuddling a cute puppy.

Bertie gaped at it. "But that's not the film I want to see," he moaned.

"Well, *we* want to see it," said Reg. "It looks nice."

"And you're a bit young for scary films," said Gran.

Dirty Bertie

Reg patted Bertie on the head. "Never mind, you'll like this one," he said. "It's a love story."

Bertie's shoulders drooped. This was going to be the worst night of his life. Reg probably thought a love story would put Gran in a romantic mood. Well, not if Bertie had anything to do with it.

They went into the cinema. Gran found three seats near the front. Bertie flopped into the seat next to her.

Reg tapped him on the shoulder. "You're in my seat," he grumbled.

"No, I'm not," said Bertie.

"You ARE," said Reg, crossly. "I want to sit next to Dotty."

"Well, so do I," said Bertie. "Why can't you sit in that seat?"

"*You* sit in that one," snapped Reg.

Dirty Bertie

The woman sitting behind them made a loud tutting noise.

"Just sit down, Reg," sighed Gran. "People are looking."

Reg sat down in a sulk. Bertie sucked his slushy drink. There wouldn't be any lovey-dovey stuff with him sitting in the middle. Gran and Reg would just have to watch the film.

The lights went down as the film began.

Dirty Bertie

CRUNCH, CRUNCH!
SLUUUURP, SLUUUURP!

A hand tapped Bertie on the shoulder. It was the woman sitting behind them. "Do you have to make that noise?" she grumbled.

"It's popcorn, I can't help it," replied Bertie.

"Well, if you must eat, do it QUIETLY," hissed the woman.

Dirty Bertie

Gran gave Bertie a look. Bertie sighed. How were you meant to eat popcorn quietly? This was no fun – and the film looked rubbish. The man and woman were on a beach with the cute puppy scampering around.

"I love you," sighed the man.

"I love you too," cooed the woman.

"Woof! Woof!" barked the cute puppy.

Bertie wished the Blob Thing would appear and gobble them up. Suddenly he had a brilliant idea. What was to stop him sneaking off to see *Return of the Blob Thing*? It was showing next door. Gran and Reg were so caught up in the film, they wouldn't even notice he'd gone.

He stood up.

"Just off to the toilet," he said.

CHAPTER 4

Bertie peeped through the door. The coast was clear. He crept into the cinema and slid into a seat on the back row. His plan had worked perfectly. Now he could sit back and enjoy the scariest film ever.

On the screen it was night time. A woman jumped into a car and locked

the doors. She was trying to escape, but
the car wouldn't start.

SHLOOP! SHLOOP! Something slimy
was moving in the woods.

BANG! Suddenly the car shook.

Bertie hid his eyes. He couldn't look –
the Blob Thing was coming…

ARGHHH! THERE IT WAS!

Bertie jumped out of his seat and fled
for the door…

Back next door, Bertie clambered over people's legs to get to his seat.

"What took you so long?" Gran whispered.

"I got lost!" said Bertie.

He went to sit down – but wait, what was this? Reg had pinched his seat!

"You're in my seat!" hissed Bertie.

"It's my seat now," replied Reg. "Sit there."

"Will you just sit down and BE QUIET!" snapped the woman behind them.

Bertie sat down next to Reg, who shot him a look of triumph.

Okay, you asked for it, thought Bertie. *This is war.*

Dirty Bertie

In the film the couple were huddled on
the sofa with the puppy. Reg pretended
to yawn. His arm crept round Gran's
shoulder. He snuggled in closer. Bertie
remembered what Darren had said about
his sister and her boyfriend. He had to do
something quickly. He smiled to himself.
Maybe some strawberry slushy would
cool things down?

Dirty Bertie

Bertie leaned across. "Anyone want a drink?" he asked.

"Ugh! No, take it away!" said Reg, pushing Bertie's hand away.

Oops! Ice-cold strawberry slushy emptied into Reg's lap. He shot to his feet as if he'd been stung.

Dirty Bertie

"YEEAARGHHHH!" he cried.

"Bertie!" groaned Gran.

"You idiot!" snarled Reg.

"It wasn't my fault!" said Bertie.

"RIGHT, THAT'S IT! I'm calling the manager!" cried the woman sitting in the row behind.

Bertie never got to see the end of *Me, You and Bonzo Too* because the manager asked them to leave. Bertie could guess what happened anyway. They got married and lived happily ever after.

Reg wasn't so happy. He drove them home in stony silence and parked outside Gran's door.

"Well, thank you, Reg," said Gran. "How are your trousers now?"

"Damp," said Reg stiffly. "I won't come in, thank you."

"Perhaps it's for the best," said Gran.

Bertie got out and waited on the pavement.

Reg sniffed. "I won't be at ballroom dancing next week, I'm taking Beryl out to dinner," he said. "Just the *two* of us."

"I see," said Gran. She got out and slammed the car door.

Bertie and Gran watched Reg drive off.

"Ah well," sighed Gran. "I was going off him anyway. I think he fancies himself."

"Yes," agreed Bertie. "He smells of cat wee too."

Gran laughed. "I think that's his aftershave," she said. "Come on, I've got some chocolate cake in the cupboard."

Bertie followed her indoors. He felt in

Dirty Bertie

his pocket. Actually, the evening hadn't
been a total disaster. Gran had bought
his ticket so he still had the five pounds
Dad had given him. And next week at
the cinema they were showing *Pirates of
Blood Island 3*...

SPLODGE!

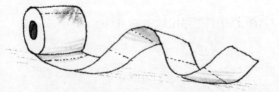

CHAPTER 1

Miss Boot seemed to be in a good mood this morning.

"I have some exciting news," she said. "Next Tuesday we are all going on a school trip."

Bertie sat up. He loved going on trips. The coach ride, the crisps and fizzy drinks, the being sick on the way home… Last term they'd gone to the zoo, which had been brilliant – apart from getting his head stuck in the bars of a monkey cage. But where was Miss Boot planning to take them this time? Maybe to the Space Centre – or, better still, to Chocolate World!

"You'll be excited to hear we are going to the City Art Gallery," said Miss Boot.

"The *art gallery*?" Bertie groaned so loudly that everyone turned round.

"Yes, the art gallery, Bertie," said Miss Boot icily. "And not just any art. We have the chance to see one of the world's greatest paintings."

She clicked on her laptop and a picture came up. It showed a bunch of flowers in a vase.

"Does anyone know this painting?"
asked Miss Boot. "Who can tell me what
it's called?"

A hand shot up. "It's *Sunflowers*, by
Van Boff," said Nick, smugly.

Trust Know-All Nick to know the answer,
thought Bertie.

"Very good, Nicholas," said Miss
Boot. "This painting belongs to a famous
gallery in London, but next week it's
coming here. You are very lucky to have

the chance to see it."

"Why's it so famous, Miss?" asked
Eugene.

"Because Van Boff was a great artist
and this is one of his finest paintings,"
said Miss Boot. "Look at it carefully
– the colours, the brushwork – it is a
masterpiece."

Bertie looked. Van Boff had certainly
used a lot of paint. But why waste it on
a bunch of droopy old flowers? If it was
Bertie's painting, he'd at least choose
something interesting – like a Tyrannosaurus
rex fighting an army of ninja robots.

He stuck up his hand. "Is it worth
anything?" he asked.

Miss Boot laughed. "It's a Van Boff,
Bertie, it's priceless."

"You mean free?"

Dirty Bertie

"I mean, it is worth millions," said Miss Boot.

Millions? Bertie's mouth fell open. People would pay a million pounds for that splodgy old flower painting? Why hadn't anyone told him this before? He'd have paid a lot more attention in art lessons! For a million pounds he'd paint anything – even Nick's ugly face. And what about the doodles inside his maths book? He'd done some great cartoons of Miss Boot. Maybe the art gallery would buy them!

$2 \times 2 = 4$
$2 \times 3 = 6$
$2 \times 4 = 10$
$2 \times 5 =$

Dirty Bertie

Back home, Bertie handed his mum a letter from Miss Boot.

"It's a school trip," he explained. "I was hoping for Chocolate World but it's an art gallery."

"The City Art Gallery?" said Mum. "Well, that could be fun."

"Hmm," said Bertie, helping himself to biscuits. "Miss Boot wants us to see some old flower painting."

Dirty Bertie

"Flower painting?" said Mum. "You don't mean Van Boff's *Sunflowers?*"

"Yes, that's it," said Bertie.

"But that's amazing," said Mum. "I was reading in the local paper that it's coming here. I've always wanted to see it."

Bertie wiped his mouth. "I don't see what the fuss is about, it's only some old picture," he said.

"It's a Van Boff," said Mum. "Do you know what that painting is worth?"

"Miss Boot says millions," replied Bertie.

"Yes, and it's world famous – everyone knows it," said Mum.

"I don't," Bertie said.

"No, but you're going to see it," said Mum. "I wish I was going. You don't know how lucky you are."

Bertie sniffed. Everyone kept telling him how lucky he was, but he'd much rather Miss Boot took them to Chocolate World. They gave away free chocolate bars to every visitor – now *that* would be lucky!

CHAPTER 2

Class 3 filed into the art gallery behind Miss Boot and Mr Weakly. They had arrived early to avoid the crowds.

"Right," said Miss Boot. "Let me remind you that this is an art gallery, not a playground. There'll be no running or fighting and no eating sweets or crisps. Most importantly, I don't want you

TOUCHING. Is that clear, Bertie?"

"Touching what?" asked Bertie.

"Touching *anything*," said Miss Boot.

Bertie sighed heavily. Why did teachers always pick on him? All he'd done was get off the coach!

Mr Weakly came round handing out some worksheets that the gallery had supplied. Bertie looked around at the paintings.

"Sir, which is the one that's worth millions?" he asked.

"The Van Boff? Ah, that's in a room by itself," said Mr Weakly. "They're letting us see it later."

Miss Boot split the class into two groups to go round the gallery. Luckily Bertie and his friends were in Mr Weakly's group. Mr Weakly was a nervous young teacher whose speech was peppered with "ahhs", "errs" and "umms". Bertie had never even heard him raise his voice – apart from the time he got locked in the store cupboard.

They wandered round the gallery, looking at the paintings. Bertie stared at a picture of people in big hats having a picnic. It made him hungry. His mum had given him some spending money and on the way in he'd spotted a gift shop. But the teachers wouldn't let him near it. Unless… Bertie had an idea. He pressed his pencil on to his worksheet.

SNAP!

That should do the trick. Now to ask Mr Weakly.

"My pencil's broken, sir," complained Bertie, holding it up.

"Oh dear!" said Mr Weakly. "Don't you have another one?"

"No," said Bertie.

"Well, ah … surely someone could lend you one?"

"They can't," said Bertie. "But it's fine, they sell pencils in the shop."

"Do they? Oh well… Mmm," said Mr Weakly. He looked round for Miss Boot, but she was nowhere to be seen.

Dirty Bertie

"I'm not sure we're allowed in the shop yet," he said.

"It's okay, it won't take a minute!" said Bertie. He hurried off before Mr Weakly could say any more. Now what could he buy with his spending money?

Dirty Bertie

"Where have you been?" asked Darren.

Bertie wiped chocolate from round his mouth.

"Gift shop," he said. "And look what I got. It was in the Bargain Bin."

He checked that no teachers were about and pulled something from his pocket.

"A WATER PISTOL!" cried Eugene.

"Shh! Keep your voice down!" hissed Bertie. "It works too. I filled it up in the boys' toilets."

"Better not let Miss Boot see it," said Darren. "She'll go mad."

Bertie looked around for a suitable victim. Now, who could he squirt? Trevor? Royston Rich? Or what about that sneaky show-off…

"I've finished!" boasted Nick, waving his worksheet. "And I bet I got them all right too."

Perfect timing, thought Bertie. He raised his water pistol and took aim.

Nick gaped at him. "Where did you get that?" he squawked.

"From the shop," smiled Bertie. "Let's see if it works, shall we?"

CHAPTER 3

"HEEEEELP!"

Nick skidded round a corner, panting for breath. Bertie raced after him, the water pistol in his hand.

"Aha! Got you now!" Bertie cried.

The room was empty.

"Keep away!" moaned Nick. "I'll tell Miss Boot!"

"She's not here," said Bertie.

"I'll scream!" wailed Nick.

"Prepare to die," said Bertie, aiming the water pistol. His finger tightened on the trigger.

SQUIRT!

At the last moment Nick ducked under a rail, escaping into a side room.

Rats! Why can't he stay still? thought Bertie. The side room was small and dimly lit. Something stood on an easel partly covered by a pair of red velvet curtains. Nick's face suddenly shot out from behind it.

"CAN'T CATCH ME!" he yelled.

SQUOOOOOOOSH!

Bertie squirted a big jet of water. He missed, hitting the red curtains instead.

Nick crept out from behind the easel.

"Umm, look what you've done!" he said.

Bertie pulled back the curtains. He gasped. Underneath was a painting he recognized straight away. Van Boff's *Sunflowers!* It was worth millions and he'd just squirted it. Water had splashed the curtain and dripped down the painting, plopping on the floor.

Nick stared, wide-eyed. "You are dead."

Dirty Bertie

"It's only water, it'll come off," said Bertie. He reached out, dabbing the wet patch with his sleeve.

"Don't touch it!" warned Nick. But it was too late. Bertie stared at the smudge of green paint on his sleeve. He gulped. This couldn't be happening! If Miss Boot found out, the art gallery would have him arrested. His mum and dad would have to sell the house and probably his sister to pay the money back.

Dirty Bertie

Nick was backing away, eager to escape. "I'm telling!" he said.

"You can't!" begged Bertie. "They'll kill me."

"You should have thought of that when you bought a water pistol," said Nick.

"If you tell tales, I'll say it was your fault," said Bertie.

"You wouldn't!"

"Try me."

Nick frowned. He didn't want to risk getting in trouble – and he shouldn't have entered the room in the first place.

"Okay, I won't tell," he said. "But the painting's your problem."

He ducked under the rail and hurried off.

Left alone, Bertie stared at the

smudged, priceless painting. Any moment now someone might come in and discover what he'd done. He had to think fast. Maybe he could hide the painting? But Mr Weakly said people were coming in to see it. If only he could make it look like new.

Bertie's eyes lit up. Of course! It was only a bunch of droopy flowers in a vase. Anyone could draw that! All he needed was paper and Eugene's felt-tip pens. By the time he'd finished, his picture would be as good as a Van Boff – probably even better! But first he had to hide the real thing.

CHAPTER 4

An hour later, Miss Boot gathered
her class together. The great moment
had arrived. The art gallery was about
to present Van Boff's *Sunflowers* in
Room 21.

"Now, follow me," said Miss Boot. "If
we hurry, we should get a good view."

They made their way to Room 21,

following people who were heading the same way. Bertie caught Nick's eye and put a finger to his lips. If they both kept their mouths shut maybe they'd come out of this alive.

They filed into the small room, which was already filling up with people. In the centre stood the priceless painting, hidden under the curtains and bathed in a spotlight. The crowd parted to let the class through to the front. Bertie wouldn't have minded staying at the back, in case he needed to make a quick exit.

The director of the gallery stepped forward. Bertie held his breath. This was it – the moment he'd been dreading!

Dirty Bertie

"Well, thank you all for coming," said the director. "This is a very proud day for the City Gallery. It is my pleasure to present one of the world's greatest masterpieces ... Van Boff's *Sunflowers*!"

She pulled on a cord and the red curtains swished back. The crowd gasped. The painting in front of them showed flowers in a vase, but it wasn't a Van Boff. It was a Van Bertie.

The flowers were messy blobs of red and brown drawn in felt-tip pen. They drooped from a vase that looked like a dog bowl. In one corner someone had signed the picture "VAN BIFF" in childish handwriting.

The director stared, holding her head. "Is this some sort of joke?" she said. "Where is the Van Boff?"

Bertie had gone bright red. It didn't look like they had got away with it. The director was phoning someone. Security guards rushed in while everyone talked at once.

Dirty Bertie

Suddenly Miss Boot stepped forward.

"Excuse me," she said. "Do you mind if I take a closer look?"

She bent over to inspect the blobby picture. Something about the style was familiar – the messy colours, the terrible handwriting. She groaned. Of course – she might have known!

Van Biff.

Dirty Bertie

"BERTIE!" boomed Miss Boot. "I want a word with you."

Uh oh, thought Bertie. How did she know it was him?

He trailed out to the front.

"Did you draw this picture, Bertie?" demanded Miss Boot.

"Me?" said Bertie. "N-no!"

"Show me your hands," ordered Miss Boot.

Bertie held them out. He had felt-tip pen on his fingers and paint on his sleeve.

Dirty Bertie

"I'll ask you one last time," said Miss Boot. "Is this your picture?"

"Um…"

"It wasn't my fault!" wailed Know-All Nick. "He chased me with a water pistol!"

Bertie rolled his eyes. Trust Know-All Nick to give the game away.

Miss Boot's eyes blazed. "Where is it, Bertie?" she thundered. "What have you done with the real Van Boff?"

Bertie swallowed hard. "Don't worry," he said. "I've hidden it somewhere really safe."

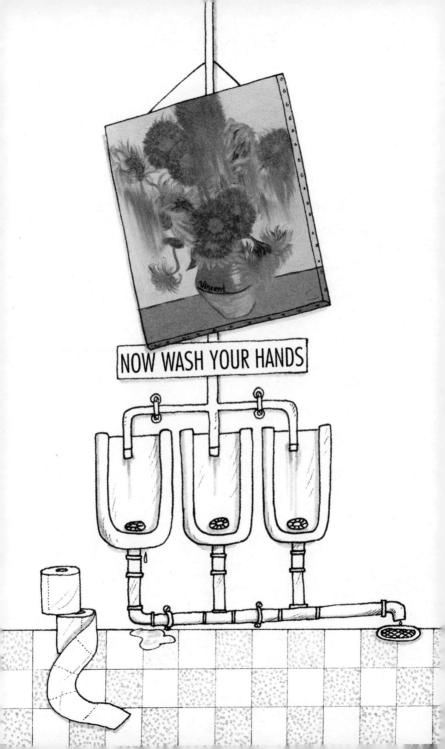

CHAPTER 1

Bertie reached up to grab his money box. There was a pirate telescope he needed to buy. With a telescope he could spy on his enemies and spot Miss Boot coming from a mile away.

He emptied out his cash.

PLINK!

Huh? Five measly pence! How come

he never had any money? It was all right for his mum and dad – they had jobs. When Bertie grew up he was going to get a job that paid a fortune. He'd be a robot scientist or a chocolate taster or maybe King of England. But the trouble was he needed money *now*.

He thought hard. Maybe he *could* get a job. What about Darren's cousin Neil? He had a paper round. If Bertie had a paper round he could buy a hundred telescopes. He'd tell Darren his idea tomorrow.

Neil went to the big school down the road. Bertie and Darren waited for him by the gates at home time.

"This is a brilliant idea," said Darren.

Dirty Bertie

"I'm saving up for a new bike."

"I'm buying a telescope," said Bertie. "Look, isn't that him?"

Neil came out of school, swinging his bag. He stopped when he saw them and listened as they explained their idea.

"A paper round? You two?" Neil laughed, shaking his head. "You've got to be thirteen at least."

"We could look thirteen," said Bertie. "Especially if we wear false beards."

"Yeah, good one!" grinned Neil. "Anyway there's nothing going, all the paper rounds are taken."

"Are you sure?" asked Darren.

"I should know," said Neil. "I had to wait six months to get one."

Bertie and Darren looked disappointed. They had raised their hopes for nothing. Now they'd never earn any money. They turned to go – but Neil stopped them.

"Tell you what," he said. "Where do you live?"

"Me? Fleaman Drive," said Bertie.

Dirty Bertie

"That's on my round," said Neil. "Listen, I'll do you a big favour. I'll pay you a pound to deliver papers to your street and Hazel Road."

"A pound EACH?" said Darren.

"Do I look stupid?" said Neil. "A pound between you, that's the deal. Take it or leave it."

Bertie and Darren stepped aside to talk it over.

"A pound? It's not very much," grumbled Darren.

"But it's better than nothing," said Bertie. "And with both of us it wouldn't take long."

"True," said Darren. "Okay, I'm in."

They told Neil they would do it.

"Great," he said. "I'll come round tomorrow and drop off the papers."

Neil watched them go, smiling to himself. For him it was *definitely* a good deal. He'd got rid of almost half of his paper round and it was only costing him one pound a week. That still left him seven pounds in his pocket. Best of all, he was losing the street that he always dreaded – Hazel Road. *Poor little kids*, he thought, *they've no idea what's in store for them.*

CHAPTER 2

Bertie arrived home and threw his bag down in the hall. He was excited about the paper round, but there was just one small problem. He hadn't actually asked his parents yet.

He found his mum emptying the washing machine.

"Mum," he began. "You know

Darren's cousin?"

"Not really," replied Mum.

"The one with big ears."

"That's half the boys you know," said Mum. "But what about him?"

"He's got us a job!" said Bertie.

Mum stared. "A job? What kind of job?" she asked.

"A paper round," said Bertie. "It's okay, we're getting paid."

"You're telling me a newsagent is paying *you* to deliver papers?" said Mum.

"Not a newsagent, Darren's cousin," said Bertie. He explained the deal they'd made with Neil. Mum frowned.

"What does Darren's mum say about this?" she asked.

"She thinks it's brilliant," said Bertie. At least she would when Darren told her.

"Hmm," said Mum. "I don't want you crossing busy roads."

"We won't have to," said Bertie. "It's only our street and Hazel Road. Anyway, I'll be with Darren."

Mum rolled her eyes. Darren was about as sensible as a chimpanzee.

Still, it might not be such a bad idea.

"Maybe it would do you good to earn some pocket money," said Mum. "You might not spend it so quickly."

"I wouldn't!" said Bertie. "I'm saving up."

Mum sighed. "All right, we'll see how it goes."

"YAY! Thanks!" cried Bertie.

"But don't go any further than Hazel Road," warned Mum.

"We won't," promised Bertie. He dashed off to phone Darren with the good news. Starting tomorrow they were going to be rich!

The next day Neil dropped off a big batch of newspapers at Bertie's house.

Dirty Bertie

Bertie and Darren stared at them.

"There's hundreds," moaned Darren.

"It'll take us forever!"

Dirty Bertie

Bertie looked at his watch. "*Danny's Deadly Dinosaurs* starts in half an hour," he said. It was his favourite programme.

Darren sighed. "We'll never make it back in time."

"We will if we get a move on," said Bertie.

They dumped out books, pens and apple cores from their school bags and divided the newspapers between them. It was a tight fit but they managed it.

Dirty Bertie

They decided to begin on Hazel Road and work back to Bertie's street.

The houses on Hazel Road had long driveways and tall iron gates. At first Bertie found the letterboxes too small, but he soon learned to roll up the newspapers. After a few houses he started to get into his stride. Across the road, he saw that Darren was keeping up. Bertie waved.

"Let's speed up!" he called. "Ten minutes to finish this road."

"Easy," said Darren. "I'm super quick."

"I'm on fire," said Bertie. If they carried on at this speed they'd be back in time to watch *Danny's Deadly Dinosaurs*.

Bertie raced to the next house, pulling a paper from his bag. There was a red car in the driveway. He weaved round it, trampling the flowerbed.

THUNK! The newspaper whizzed through the letterbox. Bertie wheeled away, taking a shortcut across the lawn. Over the road Darren was zooming in and out of driveways like a greyhound. Bertie grabbed a bunch of newspapers and flung open the next gate. A garden gnome went flying as he skidded down the path. THUNK!

At number twenty the garden wall was only knee-high. Bertie cleared it in one go. THUNK! Another paper slammed home. The next wall was bigger, but it was still quicker than taking the drive. He threw over his bag and scrambled after it…

"GRRRRRR!"

Dirty Bertie

Uh-oh. What was that? Bertie turned
round slowly. A giant dog stood there,
growling at him. It was the biggest dog he'd
ever seen – bigger than a wolf. Its ears
were folded back and its fur stood on end.
Bertie gulped. It looked like the kind of
dog that ate paper boys for breakfast.

"Good dog," he squeaked. "I won't hurt you."

"GRRRRRR… RUFF!" barked the dog. It was wearing a collar with the name 'Brutus' in big letters.

"Stay, Brutus, stay," said Bertie. "I'm just going to put this paper through the letterbox, okay?"

He bent down slowly to take a newspaper from the bag. Brutus snarled, showing rows of sharp white teeth. "GRRR!"

Bertie dropped the paper and flew back over the wall, landing in a heap.

What now? This was impossible! How was he meant to deliver the paper with a giant dog trying to eat him alive?

CHAPTER 3

Bertie stood outside the gate of number twenty-two wondering what to do. At last Darren appeared.

"What are you waiting for?" he said. "I thought we were in a hurry!"

"Never mind that," said Bertie. "There's a dog at this house."

"Oh no, NOT A DOG!" cried Darren,

pretending to tremble. "Did the nasty doggy bark at you?"

Bertie scowled. "It's a monster," he said. "I was lucky to get out alive."

Darren shrugged. "Well, as long as you delivered the paper."

"How could I?" said Bertie. "He wouldn't let me near the door."

Darren was frowning at him. "Where's your bag?" he asked.

"What?"

"The bag – with all the newspapers," said Darren.

Bertie turned round. ARGH! In his panic he must have left the bag in the driveway!

"You didn't leave it?" groaned Darren.

"It's not my fault!" said Bertie. "He was after me!"

Dirty Bertie

"But we've still got the other houses to do," said Darren. "You'll have to go back."

"Are you MAD?" cried Bertie. "Go in there?"

"It's only a dog!" said Darren. "Don't be such a baby!"

Bertie dragged Darren to the gate and pointed down the drive. Brutus was tearing a newspaper to shreds with his teeth.

"*That's* what I'm talking about," said Bertie.

"Yikes," gasped Darren. "He's ENORMOUS!"

"I know," said Bertie. "But like you say, he's only a dog, so why don't *you* get the bag?"

"No way!" said Darren. "You're the one who left it."

They stared through the gate.

Now what? thought Bertie. Without the bag they didn't have enough papers to finish the round. The shop would get complaints and Neil would hear about it. Worst of all, they wouldn't get paid. There was only one thing for it – someone had to face Brutus.

CHAPTER 4

Bertie's hands were damp with sweat. He grasped the gate. This was it, he was probably going to die. Tomorrow morning his parents would read about it in the newspaper – though not if it wasn't delivered.

"Take a stick," suggested Darren.

"To fight him off?" said Bertie.

185

"No dumbo, for him to fetch," said Darren. "When he runs after it you can grab the bag."

Bertie nodded. It was worth a try. Whiffer could never resist a stick so Brutus was probably the same. Bertie found a stick in someone's front garden. Actually it was more like a twig, but it was the best he could do.

Opening the gate, he tiptoed inside. The gate swung slowly back into place.

CLANG!

Bertie groaned. There went any chance of sneaking in quietly.

"Hurry up!" hissed Darren.

Bertie crept down the drive. "Don't panic, keep calm," he said to himself. His dad said that dogs could smell fear.

"Hi! Me again," croaked Bertie. Brutus

Dirty Bertie

rose to his feet. He seemed to have grown even bigger since last time.

"Look – STICK!" cried Bertie, holding out the twig. "You like sticks, eh?"

Brutus's tail thumped against the wall. Bertie took a step closer, breathing hard. This was near enough. He drew back his arm and threw the stick, which landed on the lawn.

"FETCH, BOY! FETCH!" cried Bertie.

Brutus turned his head, considering whether it was worth the effort.

It was now or never. Bertie darted forward and grabbed the bag of papers. Brutus snarled. Suddenly he sprang forward, seizing one of the bag straps.

Help! thought Bertie, trying to pull the

bag away.

Brutus pulled back.

"LET GO!" grunted Bertie.

"GRRR! GRRR!"

Suddenly there was a loud ripping sound as the strap came away. Bertie fell back on the drive with the bag on top of him. Newspapers flew everywhere. He felt hot smelly breath on his face and got a close-up of Brutus's teeth.

This is it, thought Bertie. *I'm dead…*

"BRUTUS! COME HERE!"

Bertie opened his eyes and sat up. A man had come out of the house. Brutus bounded over to him, wagging his tail.

"It's okay, he won't hurt you!" said the man. "He's just a big softie."

You could have fooled me, thought Bertie.

The man looked around. Bits of
newspaper littered his garden. One
page was caught in a rose bush.

"You're not the usual paper boy, are
you?" he said.

"Oh no. This is my first day," grunted
Bertie, getting to his feet.

"So I see," said the man. "Looks like
you need a bit more practice."

Dirty Bertie

About an hour later, Neil called round
to pay them their money.

"Everything go okay?" he asked. "You
get rid of all the papers?"

"Oh yes," said Bertie. They'd certainly
got rid of them all, though not always
through a letterbox. To get
back in time for *Danny's Deadly
Dinosaurs* they'd had to
finish in a hurry.

Dirty Bertie

"We ran into a bit of trouble," said
Bertie. "At number twenty-two."

Neil laughed. "Ah right, you met
Brutus then?"

"You know him?" said Darren.

"I should do, he's chased me
often enough," said Neil, grinning
at them. "Why do you think I
gave you Hazel Road?"

Bertie couldn't believe it.
Neil had known about Brutus
from the start and he hadn't even
warned them. No wonder he wanted to
get rid of half his paper round!

"Anyway, no harm done," said Neil,
handing them fifty pence each. "So same
time next week then?"

Bertie and Darren looked at each
other.

Dirty Bertie

"No thanks," said Bertie.

Neil's grin vanished. "But what about our deal – a pound a week?" he said.

"That's okay, you keep it," said Bertie. "Oh, and say hi to Brutus for me."

Bertie closed the front door. Next time he wanted a job he'd look for something safer – lion taming for instance.

Dirty Bertie

ALIENS!

For all the aliens out there ~ D R

To Jacob Moorhouse – and all at Gonville
School, Wanganui, New Zealand ~ A M

Contents

ALIENS!

CHAPTER 1

"Race you!" said Darren on the way back from school. "Last one to the corner is a dummy!"

Bertie and Eugene chased after him. But as Bertie reached the library he skidded to a halt. A large, brightly coloured poster caught his eye. It showed a picture of a flying saucer.

ALIENS
IS ANYBODY OUT THERE?

A Talk by BARRY NUTTING
(P.U.S.S. Pudsley UFO Spotters' Society)

Bertie stared. He had never been to a talk at the library. Usually they were about flower arranging or Roman pots. But aliens? That was a different matter. Bertie had seen every alien film ever made – or at least the ones his parents had let him watch. He had an alien pencil case and a poster of the planets on his bedroom wall.

Dirty Bertie

"What kept you?" panted Darren, as he and Eugene came back to join him.

"Have you seen this?" asked Bertie. "Do you think aliens really exist?"

"Probably," said Darren. "Look at Know-All Nick, he's definitely an alien."

"But *real* aliens," said Bertie.

Darren shook his head. "If they exist, how come nobody's ever met one?"

"Who says they haven't?" argued Bertie. "Maybe this Nutting guy has seen one."

Eugene was still staring at the poster. "I've never seen an alien, but I've seen planets," he said.

Dirty Bertie

"When?" asked Darren.

"Lots of times," replied Eugene. "Through a telescope."

"You've got a telescope?" said Bertie, amazed.

"It's my dad's, he got it last month," said Eugene. "He keeps it in the top room."

Bertie was impressed – a real telescope!

The only telescope he owned was a plastic pirate one with a cracked lens.

"Could I have a go on it?" he asked.

Eugene hesitated. "My dad doesn't really like people touching it – apart from me," he said.

Dirty Bertie

"I'm not going to break it," said Bertie. "I just want a little look."

"We could come round when your dad's not there," suggested Darren.

Eugene looked doubtful. "Maybe," he said. "I think he's out tonight, but we'd have to wait until it's dark."

"Great!" said Bertie. This was going to be brilliant. They could see the moon and comets and maybe a shooting star or two. Best of all, they might even see an actual UFO. Imagine that – a spaceship zooming towards Earth from a distant galaxy! Bertie got goosebumps just thinking about it.

CHAPTER 2

Later that evening, Eugene crept upstairs
with Bertie and Darren. His dad was out
at a meeting, but Eugene was worried
he might return and catch them. The
new telescope stood on a tripod by
a large window. Bertie gasped. It was
about twenty times the size of his pirate
telescope.

"It's mega!" he said, reaching out a hand.

"Don't touch!" cried Eugene. "Dad goes crazy if there are marks on the lens. He'll know I've been using it."

"Okay, keep your wig on," said Bertie.

Eugene showed them how to look through the telescope and focus on an object. Bertie couldn't wait to have a go.

"Me first," he cried.

"That's not fair! Why you?" argued Darren.

"I'm the oldest," said Bertie.

"No you're not, I am!"

Dirty Bertie

In the end they tossed a coin and Darren won. Bertie was forced to wait impatiently, listening to Darren going on about how amazing it was.

At long last it was Bertie's turn and he squinted through the lens. At first all he could see was a fuzzy pink blob, but it turned out that he was pointing the telescope at Eugene's face. Once he tilted it upwards, the night sky came into focus. He could see brilliant stars – millions of them.

Dirty Bertie

"There's the moon!" he said. "Wow! It's like a massive cheeseball!"

Bertie moved the telescope. Stars and more stars…

"WHAT WAS THAT?" he gasped.

"What?" said Eugene.

"Something just whizzed across the sky!" said Bertie. "Like a streak of light."

"Where? Let me see!" cried Eugene.

Eugene and Darren both crowded in to look, but whatever Bertie saw had vanished.

"It was probably a shooting star," said Eugene, disappointed.

Bertie shook his head. "You know what it was?" he said dramatically. "A UFO!"

"A UFO?" snorted Darren. "You mean an alien spaceship?"

"Why not?" said Bertie. "It was going like crazy."

Darren pulled a face. "You're bonkers, Bertie," he said.

Bertie ignored him and put his eye to the telescope again. A UFO – that's *exactly* what it was! A ball of light speeding like a rocket. What if it *was* an alien spaceship? Bertie's heart beat faster. What if aliens were on their way to Earth right now and he was the only one who'd seen them?

That night Bertie dreamed that aliens had invaded his school. His whole class had turned into aliens, each with the pale, ugly face of Know-All Nick.

Bertie woke up in a cold sweat. Thank goodness it was only a dream! Then he remembered the bright streak of light he'd seen through the telescope. He sat up in bed. If it *was* a UFO, he had to tell someone. Someone who knew about aliens and would believe him.

CHAPTER 3

The next morning Bertie hurried down
to the kitchen.

"Dad, can we go to the library?" he
pleaded. "There's a talk I want to hear."

Dad raised an eyebrow. A talk? At
the library? Usually on a Saturday Bertie
met his friends at the sweet shop.
Still, a talk might be educational and it

wasn't often that Bertie begged to go to the library.

When Dad and Bertie arrived, the talk on UFOs had just begun. They sat at the back and listened as a series of pictures came up on a screen. When it was over, Bertie insisted his dad wait behind while he asked Mr Nutting something. The expert was packing away his papers.

"'Scuse me," said Bertie. "Can I ask you a question?"

"Of course. Fire away, young man," said Mr Nutting.

"Have you actually met any aliens?" asked Bertie.

"Met them? Well, no!" laughed Mr Nutting. "But that doesn't mean they

don't exist. As I told you, there have
been hundreds of sightings of UFOs –
this one for instance."

He pointed to a photo of a blurry
blob, like a fried egg
in the sky. Bertie
looked closer.

"That's it, *that's*
what I saw!" he
said excitedly.

"You?"

"Yes," said
Bertie. "I was
looking through a
telescope last night and it
zoomed across the sky!"

Mr Nutting raised his eyebrows.

"Astonishing!" he said. "Well, who
knows, perhaps it *was* a UFO."

"The thing is, what do I do?" asked Bertie.

"Do?" said Mr Nutting.

"Yes – I mean if it's a spaceship and aliens have landed, how do I find them?" asked Bertie.

Mr Nutting smiled. "If I could answer that I'd be famous," he said. "The day someone makes contact with aliens will be the greatest day in history."

"REALLY?" said Bertie.

He would have liked to stay and talk, but he was in a rush to meet his friends. Taking one of Mr Nutting's leaflets, he left the library deep in thought. So it *was* an alien spaceship he'd seen – the expert had confirmed it! But where was it now? Had it landed nearby – in the woods or on the tennis courts? Either way Bertie was determined to find it. Just think, the aliens might invite him back to their planet to be King!

Outside the sweet shop, Darren and Eugene were waiting.

"Where have you been?" demanded Darren. "We've been waiting HOURS!"

"I went to the library," said Bertie. "And listen to this – that thing I saw, it *was* a UFO!"

Eugene bit in to a jelly snake. "How do you know?"

"Because I asked the UFO man," said Bertie. "He says spaceships are spotted practically every week. So, what if one has landed? What if the aliens are here *now*?"

"At the sweet shop?" asked Darren.

"NO! Anywhere!" said Bertie.

Darren sucked a toffee. "Listen, you're not going to meet any aliens," he sighed.

"Why not?" said Bertie.

"And even if it *was* a UFO you saw, how would you find it?" asked Eugene.

Bertie had thought of that. "I'm going to send the aliens a message," he said. "I'll send it tonight and then we'll see what happens!"

Darren nudged Eugene. "Maybe Bertie's right," he grinned. "You never know, the aliens might even answer."

Dirty Bertie

That evening, as it grew dark, Bertie stood in the back garden pointing a torch at the sky. He flashed it on and off several times to send a message to the alien visitors. Just to make sure, he spelled out a message in stones in the flower bed…

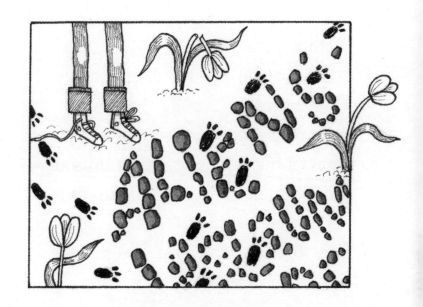

CHAPTER 4

Next morning, Bertie threw on his
clothes and hurried outside. His message
was still there but the only footprints in
the flower bed belonged to Whiffer.

Bertie trailed back inside. Surely the
aliens couldn't have missed his message?
He'd spelled it out in capital letters!
He slumped on the sofa to watch TV.

215

Dirty Bertie

DING DONG!

"Bertie, can you get that?" called Mum.

Bertie dragged himself off the sofa and went to open the door. *Yikes!* Was he dreaming? Standing outside were two actual aliens, large as life! They had green faces and enormous bug eyes, exactly like the aliens in films.

Dirty Bertie

"FLUB!" said the taller one.

"FLOB!" said the other, waving a space gun.

Bertie was so excited he could hardly speak. The aliens had answered his message – here they were, standing at his front door!

"WHO IS IT?" called Mum.

"Um … just the postman!" Bertie shouted back.

He couldn't let his mum see the aliens. She'd probably scream the house down and scare them away.

"Come in, come in!" he whispered, beckoning to them.

Bertie hurried the aliens upstairs to his bedroom and closed the door. He had so many questions he hardly knew where to start.

"Where's your spaceship? What planet are you from?" he asked. "I'm Bertie, by the way. Ber-tie."

He pointed at himself, to make them understand.

"FLIB, FLUB, FLOB!" cried his visitors, sitting down on the bed. For aliens, they seemed pretty friendly.

"This is amazing," said Bertie. "Wait till Darren and Eugene hear about this!"

Dirty Bertie

The aliens looked at each other.
Bertie's thoughts were racing. No one
was going to believe this, not unless they
saw it with their own eyes. But who
could he tell? Bertie's eye
fell on a leaflet on the
floor. Of course! Mr
Nutting – he was
an expert on stuff
like this!

"Wait here,"
Bertie told his
visitors. "I'll bring
you something to eat."

UFO ?
call NUTTING
6060 UFO !

He hurried downstairs to the phone
in the hall. Luckily Mr Nutting answered
after a moment.

"You better come quickly," said Bertie,
keeping his voice low.

"What? Who is this?" asked Mr Nutting.

"It's me, Bertie," said Bertie. "I spoke to you after your talk."

"Oh, the boy at the library," said Mr Nutting.

"Yes, but listen, I've got two aliens here – at my house!" said Bertie.

"ALIENS?" Mr Nutting snorted. "Is this your idea of a joke?"

"No, I'm serious!" replied Bertie. "I left them a message and they came."

"Look, I really don't have time for games," sighed Mr Nutting.

"Fine, don't come," said Bertie. "But if you don't, you'll be missing the greatest day in history."

Dirty Bertie

There was a long silence on the other end of the phone.

"Give me your address," said Mr Nutting at last. "I'll be there in ten minutes — and this had better not be a joke!"

Bertie returned to the aliens who were fighting on the bed. They sat up when they saw he'd brought the biscuit tin.

"Chocolate biscuits," said Bertie, miming eating. "Yum yum!"

The aliens seemed to have trouble eating the biscuits, but soon they were interrupted by the doorbell.

Bertie rushed to the top of the stairs. ARGH! His mum had beaten him to it!

She opened the front door to two

large bearded men, who seemed out of breath.

"Ah, my name's Nutting, pleased to meet you," said the UFO expert. "This is my friend Mr Potts. Your son called me."

"Bertie?" said Mum.

"Yes, is it true?" said Mr Nutting. "I thought he was making it up, but I had to see for myself. Are they upstairs?"

Dad came out of the lounge. "What's all this about?" he asked, puzzled.

"Well … the aliens!" said Mr Nutting. "Didn't Bertie tell you?"

Dad rolled his eyes. He might have known all this talk of UFOs would go to Bertie's head. Now Bertie was imagining little green men.

"BERTIE!" he yelled. "GET DOWN HERE!"

Dirty Bertie

Bertie crept slowly downstairs.

Mum folded her arms. "Aliens?" she said. "I'm told we have some in the house?"

"Mmm," said Bertie, nodding. "I um … suppose you want to see them?"

"I think we'd better, don't you?" said Mum.

Bertie disappeared. A minute later he was back with two small bug-eyed creatures.

Dirty Bertie

Mr Nutting let out a groan. "That's them? The aliens?"

"Yes," said Bertie. "They just turned up at the house."

"Did they?" said Mum. "I think I can guess why."

She pulled off the aliens' rubber masks. Darren and Eugene grinned.

"FLOB!" said Eugene.

"FLIB!" said Darren. "HA! HA! Fooled you, Bertie!"

Bertie looked stunned. How could he have been so stupid? He should have guessed it was his friends playing a trick.

Mum, Dad and the UFO spotters glared at him, waiting for an explanation.

Bertie threw up his hands helplessly. "Well, anyone can make a mistake!"

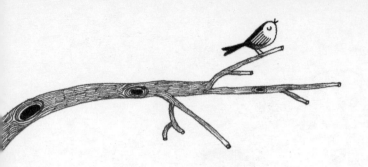

TWITTER!

CHAPTER 1

Bertie and his friends came out of the school gates. It was Friday and he was looking forward to a whole weekend without Miss Boot shouting in his ear.

"Guess what I'm doing tomorrow," said Eugene. "Birdwatching with Dad!"

Bertie raised his eyebrows. "Birdwatching?"

Dirty Bertie

"Bor-ing!" sang Darren.

"It's not!" said Eugene. "Last time we went it was the best day ever – we saw a spotted woodpecker! You have to stay really, really quiet."

"It sounds like school," said Bertie.

Eugene ignored him. "Anyway, Dad says I can bring a friend tomorrow," he went on. "So what do you think?"

Bertie looked at Darren. "US? Go *birdwatching*?" he said.

"Yes!" said Eugene. "Well, only one of you. Dad says three's too many."

Darren shook his head. "It's okay, you go, Bertie," he grinned. "I've got football practice."

"That's not fair!" grumbled Bertie. "Why do *I* have to go?"

Eugene looked hurt. "It'll be brilliant!"

he said. "Just think, a whole day out in the woods."

Bertie couldn't see what was so brilliant about it. If he wanted to watch birds he could do it from his bedroom window. In any case, birds just hopped about pecking and twittering – they didn't really *do* anything. If they had to *watch* something, what about lions or crocodiles?

"Couldn't we go to the zoo instead?" suggested Bertie.

"No, it's all arranged now," sighed Eugene. "I thought you'd *want* to come."

"He *does* want to come, don't you, Bertie?" sniggered Darren.

"Of course I do," said Bertie. "It's just … well, what would we *do* all day?"

Dirty Bertie

"There's loads to do in a wood,"
said Eugene.

This was true, thought Bertie. At
least there would be trees to climb and
branches to swing from. They could hunt
for slimy slugs or wriggly worms and
take a few home.

Dirty Bertie

"So we can run off and play?" asked Bertie.

"Maybe," said Eugene. "As long as we don't make a noise."

Bertie shrugged. "Okay, I'll think about it," he said.

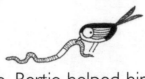

Back home, Bertie helped himself to orange juice from the fridge. His mum came into the kitchen.

"Oh, Bertie, what are you up to tomorrow?" she asked.

"I don't know yet," said Bertie. "Why?"

"Because Angela's coming round to play," replied Mum.

"ANGELA?" Bertie choked so hard that orange juice spurted out of his nose.

How could his mum do this to him?
Angela Nicely lived next door and she
was always begging to come round.
She'd probably want to play dollies' tea
parties or something. He needed to find
an excuse, and fast. But wait, he already
had one…

"Oh *tomorrow*?" he said. "I'm going
birdwatching with Eugene tomorrow."

Dirty Bertie

"Birdwatching?" said Mum. "Since when were you interested in birds?"

"Birds are very interesting actually," Bertie informed her. "If you're quiet you can see a spotty wormpecker or something."

"You mean a woodpecker," said Mum. "But can't you go another day?"

Bertie shook his head. "Sorry, it's all arranged. Eugene's dad's taking us."

Mum sighed heavily. "Very well, I'll have to put Angela off," she said. "I'm sure she'll be really disappointed."

Bertie breathed out. That was close. Even birdwatching was better than a whole day with awful Angela!

CHAPTER 2

Early the next morning, Eugene and his dad came to collect Bertie for the trip.

"Now I want you to be on your best behaviour," warned Mum. "Don't go running off."

"I won't," said Bertie.

"And no fighting or rolling in the mud," said Mum.

"I won't," said Bertie.

"And remember your please and thankyous," said Mum. "Be polite to Mr Clark."

"I won't," said Bertie, who wasn't really listening. Honestly, the way his mum went on, you would think he was meeting the Prime Minister.

He climbed into the back of the car beside Eugene and they set off.

"Well?" said Mr Clark. "I hope you're as excited as Eugene."

"Um … yes, I can't wait," replied Bertie.

"Bertie's never been birdwatching before," explained Eugene.

"*Really?*" said Mr Clark, as if this was astonishing news. "Well, you're in for a treat. Last time we saw a chiffchaff and two nuthatches, didn't we, Eugene?"

Dirty Bertie

"Yes," said Eugene. "And don't forget the woodpecker!"

"Show Bertie the book I got you," said Mr Clark.

Eugene pulled out a book from his rucksack. It was called *The Little Bird Spotter's Guide*.

Bertie turned the pages. He never knew there were so many birds! There were millions of them – big, small, speckled, long-legged, beaky and beady-eyed.

Dirty Bertie

Bertie pointed to the picture of a bird with a sharp, hooked beak.

"Wow! This one looks mean!" he said.

"That's a hawk, they're birds of prey," said Eugene. "They swoop down and catch mice and stuff. Sometimes they even carry off other birds."

Bertie's eyes widened. This sounded more like it. He wouldn't mind spotting a mean killer hawk!

"Will we see one today?" he asked.

Dirty Bertie

"I doubt it!" laughed Mr Clark. "You don't get many hawks in Fernley Woods. Anyway, we're looking for something else."

"The marsh warbler," said Eugene, nodding.

"They're pretty rare, but one was sighted recently," said his dad. "If we're very quiet and really patient we might just get lucky."

Eugene showed Bertie a picture of the marsh warbler. It was a fat little greeny-brown bird with a white chest. Bertie hardly glanced at it. He'd much rather see a killer hawk swooping down from the sky. One day he was going to get a pet hawk and train it to attack his enemies. Imagine Miss Boot's face when she was suddenly carried off in the middle of assembly.

CHAPTER 3

PLOP, PLOP, PLOP!

The rain pitter-pattered on the roof of the bird hide. Bertie passed the binoculars back to Eugene. They'd been watching the woods for HOURS, but all they'd seen was trees, bushes and pouring rain.

The hide was a bit like a garden shed

240

only bigger and colder. There were
hard benches to sit on and long narrow
windows to look out of. Eugene's dad
said that the idea was to stay hidden so
they wouldn't frighten the birds away.
Not that there *were* any birds. Bertie
was beginning to think they'd all gone on
holiday.

"See anything?" asked Mr Clark.

Eugene shook his head.

"Wait, there *is* something!" he
whispered. "Look – under the tree!"

His dad peered through the
binoculars.

"Ah yes, it's a sparrow," he said.
"Never mind."

Even Bertie knew that sparrows were
not rare birds.

"How much longer?" he groaned.

Mr Clark shot him a look.

"You must learn to be patient, Bertie," he said. "It's all about keeping your eyes open."

"Can't we have lunch?" moaned Bertie.

"We just got here! It's only eleven o'clock," said Mr Clark.

"But I'm STARVING!" cried Bertie.

Mr Clark shook his head. It was nice for Eugene to bring a friend, but he was starting to wish it wasn't Bertie. The boy had no interest in nature at all. Worse still, he never stopped talking, fidgeting or picking his nose.

Mr Clark dug into his bag and brought out a strange-looking whistle.

"I thought I might try this – it's a bird-caller," he explained. "It attracts birds because they think they hear another bird calling."

He raised the bird-caller to his lips and blew gently.

"Throop-oo! Throop-oo!"

"Amazing!" said Eugene. "It sounds just like a bird!"

"Can I have a go?" asked Bertie.

"Er … maybe it's better if I do it," said Eugene's dad.

"Pleeeeease! Just one little go," begged Bertie. "I'm not going to break it!"

Mr Clark smiled weakly and handed him the bird-caller. Bertie thought it might attract a passing hawk, looking for mice or weasels. He stood on the bench and blew a deafening blast.

"THROOP-OOO! THROOP-OOOOO!"

"Okay, that's enough now," said Mr Clark hastily.

But Bertie didn't stop.

"THROOP-OO! THROOP-OO! THROOP— URGH!"

Mr Clark snatched the bird-caller from his mouth.

"I said that's enough!" he snapped. "You'll scare every bird in the wood. Now *please* sit still and keep quiet!"

Bertie slumped on to the bench. He was only trying to help – you'd think that Eugene's dad would be grateful! He picked up an empty plastic cup and put it between his teeth.

Dirty Bertie

"What am I?" he asked Eugene.

"Dunno," laughed Eugene. "A nutcase."

"A HAWK!" cried Bertie.

He flapped his arms and swooped down upon Eugene. They both fell off the bench and rolled on the floor, giggling.

"For the last time, STOP IT!" yelled Mr Clark, losing patience. "Eugene, I'm surprised at you. Do you want to see a marsh warbler or not?"

Eugene got up. "Sorry, Dad," he mumbled.

Bertie sighed heavily. He wished the stupid bird would turn up soon, then they could all go home!

CHAPTER 4

Bertie jiggled his legs. He'd drunk all his lemonade and now he was desperate for the loo, but Eugene's dad wanted them to keep watch in silence.

"'Scuse me!" whispered Bertie.

"SHHH!" hissed Mr Clark.

"I can't shhh!" moaned Bertie. "I need the toilet!"

Dirty Bertie

"There isn't one," said Mr Clark.

"Go in the woods, that's what I always do," suggested Eugene.

"Fine," said his dad. "But don't go far and DON'T make any noise!"

Bertie hurried to the door. It was no wonder that not many children went birdwatching, he thought. If they added a café, toilets and maybe a zip wire then more people might come.

He ducked out of the hide and looked around for somewhere to go. There was a rough path leading off into the woods. Bertie followed it, half walking and half running. It wasn't easy to hurry quietly.

At last he reached a muddy bank by a pool of water. There were plenty of trees around and no one about.

Bertie closed his eyes and let out
a long sigh of relief. Then he heard
something – singing.

A fat little bird with a white front
sat on a branch twittering away. Bertie
watched it hop down to the water's
edge. He dug in his pocket and found a
few crisps that he'd been saving for later.
He scattered them on the ground.

"Here, birdy birdy!" he called softly.
"Look – crisps!"

The fat little bird hopped closer until
it was only a few steps away. Bertie kept
as still as a statue. Finally the bird pecked
at a crisp.

Bertie watched it for a minute or
two. It was quite a nice bird, even if it
wasn't a killer hawk. Finally it flew away,
vanishing into the treetops.

Dirty Bertie

"Bye-bye, birdy!" called Bertie, with a
wave.

Back at the hide, Bertie crept in the
door. Eugene and his dad hadn't moved
from their posts.

"Better?" whispered Eugene.

"Yes thanks," said Bertie. "There's
loads of trees we could climb, and guess
what — I saw a bird!"

"What kind of bird?" asked Eugene.

"Dunno, just a small one," replied
Bertie.

"Probably a sparrow," said Eugene.

"No, this was fatter," said Bertie. "Sort
of a greeny-brown colour."

Mr Clark looked at him, gripping his
binoculars.

"What colour chest did it have?" he demanded.

"White, I think," said Bertie. "It was singing."

Mr Clark turned pale. He grabbed *The Little Bird Spotter's Guide* and turned the pages.

"Think! Was it anything like this?" he asked, pointing to a picture.

"YES!" cried Bertie. "That's the one! That's it exactly!"

Mr Clark closed his eyes. "A marsh warbler!" he moaned. "You saw a marsh warbler. YOU!"

"That's good then," said Bertie. "It ate my crisps."

Bertie thought Mr Clark would have been pleased, but he didn't look it. He paced up and down, waving his hands in the air.

"UNBELIEVABLE!" he fumed. "You talk, you fidget, you blunder off into the woods and what happens? You see a marsh warbler. You, of all people!"

"Anyway," said Bertie. "Now I've seen it, can we go home?"

Mr Clark insisted they return to the spot where Bertie had seen the rare bird. They waited for another hour, but the marsh warbler didn't come back.

Mr Clark drove them home in silence. He seemed to be sulking. Bertie couldn't see what he was so cross about. After all, it wasn't *his* fault that no one else saw the marsh warbler! Besides, it was only a bird! If he'd seen a crocodile, *that* would have been something to get excited about.

Dirty Bertie

Back home, Mum let him in and made him take off his muddy boots in the hall.

"So how was birdwatching?" she asked.

Bertie shrugged. "Okay," he sighed. "But it'd be better if they had slides or a zip wire."

"I hope you behaved yourself," said Mum.

"Of course," said Bertie. "I hardly said a word all day!"

In any case, he didn't think he'd be invited to go again, which was probably just as well.

Better still, he had avoided a whole

day of Angela Nicely. That would have
been torture! And there was still an hour
to watch TV before suppertime. He
opened the lounge door.

"HI, BERTIE!" sang a voice that made
his heart sink. "Your mum said I could
come for supper! Isn't that nice?"

Bertie groaned. NOT ANGELA!
Life was so unfair!

REPORT!

CHAPTER 1

Bertie was on his way home from school
with Darren and Eugene. He took out
a large brown envelope from his bag
and stared at it for the hundredth time.
Inside was the thing he dreaded every
year – his school report. He hadn't read
it yet because mean old Miss Boot had
sealed the envelope.

Dirty Bertie

Why do teachers have to write reports anyway? thought Bertie. *Why don't children write reports on their teachers? That would be much fairer!* He knew exactly what he'd say…

Miss Boot is the wurst teacher in the univers. She is bad tempered, grouchy and canot spell for tofee.

Eugene shook his head. "There's no point staring at it," he said.

"I just want to *know*," grumbled Bertie. "It's *my* report so why can't I see it?"

"Because you're not allowed," replied Eugene. "Miss Boot said we have to give it to our parents."

Darren raised an eyebrow. "But Miss Boot's not here, is she?" he said.

Bertie looked round to check their teacher wasn't hiding behind a lamp post. You could never be too sure. He fingered the envelope.

"Shall I?" he asked.

"Go on," said Darren. "Let's all open them together!"

"We can't!" moaned Eugene. "We'll get in trouble!"

"Not if we're careful," said Bertie. "If we stick the envelope back down, who's going to know?"

Eugene looked worried, but he was dying to see his report just like the others.

Very carefully, Bertie unsealed his envelope, taking care not to tear it.

Dirty Bertie

He took a deep breath and pulled out his report. Miss Boot's spidery handwriting filled the page…

The others opened their reports.

"Phew!" said Eugene. "Mine's pretty good! It says 'Eugene is very hard-working'."

"And mine's not so bad," said Darren. "What about you, Bertie?"

Bertie looked up. "Terrible!" he groaned. "Listen to this: 'Bertie is messy, idle and never listens. If anything, his work has gone backwards this year, which is quite an achievement!'"

Darren laughed. "You *always* get a bad report," he said.

"It's not funny!" said Bertie. "The last one was so terrible I had to promise my mum that I'd improve this year. Otherwise she's going to find me a tutor!"

"*A tutor?*" repeated Darren.

"You mean, like your own teacher?" said Eugene.

"Exactly!" said Bertie.

It was bad enough seeing teachers at school without one turning up at your house. There'd be no more TV, going to the park or having fun. His life would just be work, work, work from morning till night.

No, thought Bertie, it was too horrible to imagine. He had to make sure his parents never set eyes on the report. But how? As soon as he got home, his mum would want to read it.

Bertie frowned. Wait a moment – what if his report never reached home? What if he accidentally lost it? He looked around and spotted a red postbox up ahead. Perfect! If he posted the report he'd never see it again – it would be gone forever!

He slipped the report back in the envelope and marched up to the postbox.

"What are you doing?" asked Eugene.

"I'm posting it," replied Bertie.

Dirty Bertie

"YOU CAN'T DO THAT!" cried Eugene.

"Why can't I?" said Bertie.

Before they could stop him, he pushed the envelope into the slot…

FLUMP!

It disappeared.

"Bye-bye, report!" said Bertie, patting the postbox on the head.

CHAPTER 2

Darren shook his head. "You nutter!" he laughed. "What did you do that for?"

"Miss Boot's going to kill you!" said Eugene.

"She'll never find out," said Bertie. "My address isn't even on the envelope."

"But what about your mum and dad?" asked Eugene. "They'll be expecting it."

Dirty Bertie

"No they won't," argued Bertie. "They don't even know we've got our reports."

"They'll find out when they go to Parents' Evening," said Darren.

Bertie stared. "To... What?"

"Parents' Evening," repeated Darren. "It's this Friday, remember?"

Bertie's legs turned to jelly. How could he have forgotten Parents' Evening? Miss Boot had gone on and on about it when she was handing out their reports. It was on Friday – the day after tomorrow!

"Miss Boot always talks about our reports with our parents," said Eugene. "That's what Parents' Evening is for."

"Yeah, so how are you going to explain that yours has disappeared?" asked Darren.

Bertie looked at the postbox in

horror. ARGH! What had he done? He had to get his report back or he was in serious trouble!

He peered into the mouth of the postbox.

"It's too late now," said Darren. "You'll never get it back."

Bertie wasn't listening. He squeezed his hand through the hole and felt around.

"I can't reach it!" he wailed.

"You've got no chance," said Eugene. "Just leave it!" But Bertie wasn't giving up that easily. He wriggled his arm in up to the elbow and fished around inside. It was no use.

Dirty Bertie

"Well, don't just stand there!" he grumbled. "Help me!"

"HEY YOU! GET AWAY FROM THERE!"

Bertie looked round. Yikes! It was the postman! He was getting out of his van and coming towards them. Bertie yanked his arm free so quickly that he almost fell flat on his back.

The postman set down his sack and glared.

"What do you think you're doing?" he demanded.

"Sorry," mumbled Bertie. "I lost my report."

"Your what?"

"My report, from school," explained Bertie. "I sort of, um … accidentally posted it."

The postman stared.

"You *accidentally* posted it?"

Bertie nodded. "Yes, it was a mistake, but now I need it back."

Dirty Bertie

The postman shook his head and took out a bunch of keys to unlock the postbox.

"Well, it's too late now," he said, opening his sack.

"But can't you look for it?" pleaded Bertie. "It's in a big brown envelope."

"There are hundreds of envelopes, and once they're in the box I've got to collect them," said the postman. "I can't go rummaging around."

Bertie watched helplessly as the pile of letters disappeared into the sack.

POST

"Please!" he begged. "If I don't get it back, Miss Boot will kill me."

"You should have thought of that before," said the postman. "Now I've got to get on. And in future, keep your hands out of the postbox."

He dumped the sack into the back of his van, slammed the door and drove off. Bertie watched the van disappear along with his last hope. He was done for. What on earth was he going to do?

CHAPTER 3

Back home, Bertie tried to slip in quietly and sneak upstairs.

"BERTIE? Is that you?" called Mum from the lounge.

"Um … it might be," replied Bertie.

Mum appeared in the doorway. "What are you up to?" she asked. Bertie wasn't usually quiet when he came in.

Dirty Bertie

"Nothing!" said Bertie. "I'm just going to get changed."

"Well, there are clean clothes on your bed," said Mum. "But save them for Friday – it's your Parents' Evening."

Bertie groaned. He was hoping his mum might have forgotten, but no such luck. Any minute now she'd probably ask if he'd got his school report. If only he could borrow one – Know-All Nick's for instance. He *always* got a glowing report.

Suddenly Bertie's face lit up with an idea. What if he wrote his *own* report? Then he could have the report he deserved.

Bertie has amazed evrywon this yeer. he is a shyning eggsample to his klass – and speshlly to that fat head No-All Nick. ✦ ✦ ✦

Dirty Bertie

Ten minutes later Bertie came downstairs, holding a large envelope in his hand.

"What's that?" asked Mum.

"This? It's my report," said Bertie. "Miss Boot gave them out today."

Mum took the envelope. "Well, I hope it's a lot better than your last one," she said grimly. "You remember what I told you?"

Bertie remembered only too well. Mum studied the report and frowned at him.

"Miss Boot wrote this?" she said.

Bertie nodded. "Um … yes, is it all right?"

"It's more than all right," said Mum. "Miss Boot is singing your praises."

"Is she?" said Bertie. "I guess it must be cos I've been working hard and paying attention and stuff."

"Have you now?" said Mum, narrowing her eyes.

Dad came into the lounge.

"Bertie's got his report," Mum told him.

"Oh yes?" said Dad. "What's it like?"

"Well, Miss Boot claims that he is 'dead clever' and 'top of the class'," said Mum.

Dad looked astonished. "*Seriously?*" he said, taking the report.

Bertie didn't see why everyone sounded so shocked. He'd have thought they would be delighted with his progress. Dad was reading the report for himself.

Dirty Bertie

"Class is spelt with a 'K'," he said.

"Yes," said Mum. "And I can hardly read Miss Boot's handwriting. You would *almost* say it was as bad as Bertie's writing."

"Hmm, funny that," said Dad, raising his eyebrows.

Mum folded her arms. "Well, I shall look forward to discussing this report with Miss Boot," she said.

Bertie almost choked. Miss Boot? If she saw the report she'd guess who had written it in three seconds. Worse still, she'd want to know what had happened to the REAL report.

"Oh ... um ... didn't I say?" spluttered Bertie. "Miss Boot said she can't come to Parents' Evening."

"Can't come? Why not?" demanded Mum.

"Because she's ... she's sick," said Bertie, thinking quickly. "She lost her voice from shouting at Darren so much."

"When did this happen?" asked Dad.

"Today!" said Bertie. "She was shouting, then suddenly her voice went and she said she can't come to Parents' Evening."

"I see," said Mum. "And how did she tell you that if she'd lost her voice?"

Dirty Bertie

Bertie gulped. "She um … she wrote it on the board," he said.

Mum and Dad exchanged looks.

"Well, I'm sure the school will let us know," said Mum. "I think we'll take a chance and go along anyway."

"NO!" squawked Bertie. "I mean … you'd just be wasting your time."

Mum gave him a long hard look. "We are going, whether you like it or not, Bertie," she said. "Anyone would think you had something to hide."

CHAPTER 4

Friday came round all too soon.
Bertie found himself sitting outside his
classroom, watching the clock tick by.
He had been to the toilet three times
already. He could hear Miss Boot's voice
booming like distant thunder. Know-All
Nick was in there with his parents. Bertie
was next on the list.

Dirty Bertie

"Well, it sounds like Miss Boot's got her voice back," said Dad.

"Mmm," said Bertie faintly. "Actually I feel a bit sick. Maybe I should lie down?"

"You'll live," said Mum. "Our appointment's in five minutes."

Bertie glanced down at the report poking out of his mum's bag. As soon as Miss Boot saw it he would be dead meat.

Just then the classroom door opened. Know-All Nick appeared with his parents. Nick's mum saw Bertie's mum and smiled.

Dirty Bertie

"I *do* enjoy these Parents' Evenings, don't you?" she trilled. "Such a pleasure to hear how *well* Nicholas is doing."

"Yes," replied Bertie's mum. "We can't wait to discuss Bertie's report."

Nick glowed with pride. "Miss Boot says I'm her star pupil," he boasted. "What did your report say, Bertie?"

"Mind your own business," Bertie replied.

"Never mind," jeered Nick. "Someone has to come bottom of the class. HAW HAW HAW!"

"For your information, I wasn't bottom, I came top," said Bertie.

"LIAR!" snorted Nick. "I *always* come top."

Dirty Bertie

"Not this time, smarty pants," said Bertie.

"We'll see about that," said Nick. "You better not keep Miss Boot waiting! I'm sure she's got *lots* to tell you."

Bertie breathed in. This was it. There was no escape. He followed his mum and dad into the classroom.

Miss Boot sat waiting at her desk with her mark book open.

"Ah, do come in and take a seat!" she smiled. "I've been looking forward to this."

Dirty Bertie

Bertie sat down beside his parents. His hands were sweating. He tried not to look at his teacher.

"So I take it you didn't receive Bertie's report?" said Miss Boot.

"Oh yes, we got it all right," said Mum.

"You did?" Miss Boot sounded surprised.

"Well, he gave us *a* report," said Mum. "This one."

She took out the fake report from her bag and handed it over. Miss Boot read it and her eyebrows hit the ceiling. She read out her teacher's comment:

Bertie is ded clever. This year he woz easy top of the klass.

Bertie turned red as Miss Boot fixed him with a glare. "You wrote this drivel,

284

did you, Bertie?" she said.

"M-me?" mumbled Bertie.

"Yes, YOU!" snapped Miss Boot.

"Did you really think you had us fooled for even a minute?" asked Dad.

Bertie shook his head dumbly.

"So where is your actual report?" asked Mum.

"Oh, I can answer that," smiled Miss Boot, reaching for a brown envelope. "Fortunately your report has turned up safe and sound."

Bertie went pale. *What?* It couldn't have! He'd seen the postman put it in his sack!

"It seems someone posted it," Miss Boot went on. "But the Post Office recognized the school's name and sent it back. Wasn't that a stroke of luck, Bertie?"

Dirty Bertie

Bertie slid down lower in his seat. It was so unfair! They could have sent the report anywhere — India, Australia, the North Pole — anywhere but back to his school!

Miss Boot leaned forward and smiled cruelly. "Now," she said. "Would you like to hear what *I* wrote about Bertie?"

Out now!

DAVID ROBERTS WRITTEN BY ALAN MACDONALD

Dirty Bertie

SPIDER!